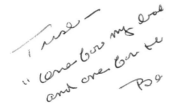

"*A charming and altogether original Christmas tale.*"

Rick Kogan
Chicago Tribune

"*Whimsical, charming and refreshing. Would make a fine film.*"

Ann Gerber
Inside Publications

"'*The Santa Claus Trial*' *is a mixture of politics, fantasy and fun.*"

Nikki Arseneau
Southtown Star

"*Not since 'Miracle on 34th Street' has there been as refreshing Christmas story as this one. Only my friend Allen would dare mix politics and Santa Claus in the same story. But he carries it off with great humor and elan.*"

Lloyd Weston, former Managing Editor
Pioneer Press

"*My husband and I enjoyed reading every page. You really brightened our day. Keep writing.*"

Helen Reimherr
Springfield, Virginia

The Santa Claus Trial
Second Edition

Allen Rafalson
Illustrated by Alex Ruiz

The Santa Claus Trial
is available online
at
www.thesantaclaustrial.com

Illustrations by Alex Ruiz

Book editing by Susan Nelson

Book design by Phil Moy

Copyright © 2013 by Allen Rafalson, 2nd Edition

U.S. Copyright Office: TXu 1-768-785

All characters appearing in this work are fictitious. Any resemblance to real persons, living or dead, is purely coincidental.

All rights reserved. No part of this publication may be reproduced, stored in a retrieval system, or transmitted, in any form or by any means, electronic, mechanical, photocopying, recording or otherwise, without prior permission from the author or publisher.

ISBN: 978-0-9852702-4-7

Paperback publishing by Prompt Graphics, Chicago

Printed in the USA

In memory of my mentor,
William P. Walsh

"Imagination is more important than knowledge."

Albert Einstein

CONTENTS

Chapter 1   1
Imagine a Christmas without Santa Claus

Chapter 2   8
Bill Camper's Childhood

Chapter 3   13
Senator McGreedy's Secret Meeting

Chapter 4   16
Growing Up with the Greedy McGreedy

Chapter 5   21
Santa Receives a Subpoena

Chapter 6   25
Camper Visits Senator Rightman

Chapter 7   30
The Santa Claus Conspiracy

Chapter 8   39
Camper Seeks Funding for North Pole Trip

Chapter 9   46
The Flight to the North Pole

Chapter 10   53
Getting Ready

Chapter 11   56
A Tour of Santa's Workshop

Chapter 12   61
A Conversation with Santa

Chapter 13   68
Santa Arrives in Washington, D.C.

Chapter 14   74
Santa's Testimony Begins

Chapter 15   91
Senator Rightman Defends Santa Claus

Chapter 16   101
The Santa Revolution

Chapter 17   109
A Moment of Truth

Chapter 18   114
Albert Hubka's Demise

Chapter 19   121
President Trublood Confronts McGreedy

Chapter 20   127
Here We Come A-Caroling

Chapter 21   132
The Beginning of the End

Chapter 22   144
The Blessing

The Santa Claus Trial

"Meet Bill Camper"

Chapter 1

Imagine a Christmas without Santa Claus

Bill Camper suddenly awoke from a deep sleep early this cold, wintry, early December, 2019 morning. He had dreamed Americans would be celebrating the Christmas holiday without Santa Claus.

"Unthinkable," he said to himself. "Celebrating this joyous holiday without Santa? Many millions of children waking up and finding their stockings empty and fewer gifts under the Christmas tree?"

"Ridiculous," he scoffed as he arose from his bed where his wife, Kate, lay asleep. She was obviously tired, for both had spent the night before busily shopping at Holman's department store purchasing a few additional Christmas presents for their two children, Sara, 7 and Brandon, 11. Besides, Kate, an attorney, had spent an exhausting day in court defending a client.

There was good reason for Camper to believe that his nightmare would come true.

The nation's elections in 2016 had brought with them a different political power, the New Party.

The Santa Claus Trial

Senator Travis McGreedy led the charge of a party that now controlled both the Senate and the House of Representatives. During the campaign the New Party had promised to improve conditions for many Americans. None of those promises were kept, despite the growing number of jobless people and families losing homes they could no longer afford to keep. The homeless lined up evenings outside soup kitchens nationwide, where they would get free meals served by volunteers.

The New Party's Morton Trublood rode Senator McGreedy's coattails and was elected President. He was a former congressman who could impress you with his speeches, but he was indecisive and looked to McGreedy, the Senate Majority Leader, for continued support.

Camper, a popular reporter for Chicago's *Daily Sunlight* whose syndicated column appeared on the Internet and in 82 other newspapers across the county, heard that McGreedy was illegally working closely with the Toymakers and Retailers Association of America (TRAA) to discredit Santa Claus. But where was the proof? Would anyone come forward and be a witness?

The rumor was already making the rounds among Washington's circle of politicians, especially now that the House of Representatives was about to vote on a Santa Tariff Act, which seemed intended to make it impossible for him to bring his toys to American homes on Christmas Eve. It was expected to pass and move on to the Senate for final approval. President Trublood had told Congress he would sign this unprecedented bill.

TRAA members were frustrated by fierce competition from companies in China where such products as toys, computers, and appliances had long been produced at lower costs. Manufacturers belonging to the association said their profits were dwindling because of the competition they faced from Santa. The nation's store owners agreed. They looked to Senator McGreedy to turn the tide by creating a tariff that would make it impossible for Santa to afford bringing his presents into the United States on Christmas Eve. McGreedy had the necessary votes.

His plan was to make Santa pay a $1.00 tax on every present he brought into the country. McGreedy knew the jolly old man did not have the huge amount of money required. With Santa out of the way, U.S. toy manufacturers and store owners could see sales and profits soar as families would have to purchase additional gifts for their children to make up for his absence.

Camper gave a big yawn as he stretched, tied a knot around his robe, and proceeded downstairs in his modestly furnished two-story home in a southwest suburb of Chicago.

How could he stop Congress from passing such an unreasonable bill, especially now, just weeks from

The Santa Claus Trial

"McGreedy, I'm going to stop you!"

Christmas?

Outside his window he could see snowflakes showering the streets and noticed ice forming on the branches of trees as they waved back and forth in the cold bristling wind … as if in prayer. He thought somehow, they too must know and would miss seeing Santa's reindeer skimming their branches as they flew from one house to another.

Camper pounded his fist on the windowsill and shouted, "McGreedy, I'm going to stop you!"

Chapter 2

Bill Camper's Childhood

Bill was the youngest of four Camper children who grew up in a comfortable three-bedroom bungalow located on Chicago's South Side neighborhood where many Irish American families chose to settle. There were also Meaghan, Tom, and Jack Jr., the oldest brother. Camper's father, Jack Sr., worked in a steel mill located along the Indiana border, an hour's car ride away. His mother, Margaret, remained at home.

It wasn't unusual for Jack Sr., a tall, friendly giant of a man, to stop by the local tavern after work and share a few beers with his buddies. Neither was it unusual for him to arrive home some evenings tipsy as dinner was served. The children were accustomed to his occasional late appearances and would giggle as their father, wearing wrinkled blue jeans and red suspenders strapped over his frequently worn blue shirt, struggled to sit down at the dinner table. Margaret was not amused.

After graduating from high school in the mid-1960s, Margaret had gotten a job as a sales clerk at Holman's department store, where she met Jack; soon afterward they got married. She left her job at the well-known neighborhood store after giving birth to Jack Jr. in 1971. The other children were born in quick succession.

Margaret wanted all her children to succeed and made sure they did their homework every day. If you get good grades, she repeated frequently, you'll be able to go to a college, graduate, get a nice job, and live in a good neighborhood.

Jack Sr. spent most of his Saturdays either doing chores around the house or working on the family's vintage white four-door Rambler. Afterward, he paid a visit to the local tavern on Saturdays and Sundays. Margaret prohibited him from driving the car weekends because she was afraid he might get into an accident after departing from the tavern. She had bought him a bicycle instead.

In the summer he would ride the bike to the pub wearing blue jeans, a T-shirt, and a Chicago White Sox baseball cap. In the cool fall weather he pedaled through the neighborhood with the top of his white winter underwear showing, his black wool pants held up tightly by his suspenders.

"Hi ya, Paddy," Jack would say whenever he passed Patrick O'Brien's house on Sundays, always tipping his cap. O'Brien, his neighbor, also worked in the mill. It wasn't unusual to see him and his wife, Mary, on weekends taking care of their beautiful bed of flowers and manicured lawn that would usually win the annual award for the community's "Best Landscaped House." "Aye, Jack!" he would shout back, tipping his Chicago Cubs cap. "See ya there soon!"

Like Margaret, Mary O'Brien, who worked part-time at the local library, was not happy about her husband's weekend romps with Jack.

Saturdays were set aside by Margaret for shopping with her children, topped off by a visit to the nearby ice cream parlor. Sunday mornings were reserved for church services and the number of charitable committees she belonged to. Tom had become an altar boy. Raising four children on Jack's modest income meant that the Campers had to spend their money wisely and, at the same time, provide a comfortable and happy home.

There were many joyful Christmas mornings. Each year it was a time for the family to sit around their large, fresh green tree decorated with colorful tinsel and ornaments. The parents proudly watched their children unwrap gifts, some left by Santa, others purchased at Holman's. Although there was no fireplace mantel to hang the colorful holiday stockings on, Margaret made sure their shoes were at the bottom of their respective stockings and in a place for all to see.

Perhaps the most memorable Christmas morning occurred in 1984. Still clad in their pajamas,

The Santa Claus Trial

"See ya there soon!"

the four opened their neatly wrapped holiday packages.

"Wow!" Jack Jr. exclaimed. "Santa left me a baseball bat and outfielder's glove. Thanks," he said. "I needed this for the high school tryouts." A freshman, he knew his parents were proud of his athletic ability.

Among Meaghan's gifts were a black and white polka-dotted dress and a new pair of shoes. Meaghan wondered how Santa knew she wanted that dress. "He even knew my size!" Margaret said she did not know the answer. But weeks before, Meaghan had seen the dress on display in Holman's store window and told her mother how much she would like to wear it for the holidays.

Tom, an ardent reader, was the recipient of two adventure books, a pair of shoes, a dress shirt and a thin red tie. Bill's gift was a portable typewriter with a note attached. It read: "Bill, I think you're going to need this in the very near future. Get used to it! Santa Claus"

Even though there was no fireplace to gather before on Christmas mornings, plenty of warmth resonated throughout the Camper household every year.

The years flew by quickly and Meaghan and Bill graduated from college. She became a schoolteacher and the mother of two children, while Bill became an award-winning journalist at one of the city's leading newspapers, the *Daily Sunlight*. Tom became a priest,

Chapter 3

Senator McGreedy's Secret Meeting

What caused Senator McGreedy to bring up a bill that would prove to be too costly for Santa? It was simply—you guessed it—greed!

Unknown to others, the senator had secretly met with high-ranking members of the Toymakers and Retailers Association of America at Hilton Head, South Carolina. They treated him with all sorts of gifts, golf games with the association president, body massages at the hotel, and plenty of exclusive lunches and dinners.

The TRAA president, Marty Mischief, is a tall, distinguished man in his 50s with silver hair and handsome features—someone you would think by appearance demanded respect. But there were rumors he had connections with members of the Mafia.

"All of us like Santa Claus, but he is too much of a threat," Mischief told McGreedy. "Retailers have been reducing their inventories in recent years because they have to compete with that old man. Many of our members are owners of plants that manufacture toys and have had to fire people because they're not getting the orders from those stores. It's not only happening in the U.S. but in countries overseas as well. It's time to

The Santa Claus Trial

"I'm going a step further!"

stop that bearded old man!" Mischief growled.

The senator, overwhelmed by his warm reception these past several days, assured everyone that the bill would pass, adding that President Trublood was on his side and that his New Party had enough votes to override the anticipated public discontent.

It was now time for McGreedy to return to the Capitol Building in Washington, D.C. The senator, who always packed lightly, was now carrying a heavy piece of luggage bulging with the numerous presents he had just received from TRAA during his three-day junket.

He was escorted to the airport by several members of TRAA. Just before he boarded the plane, he told them that he had another plan. "What is it?" they asked.

"I'm going a step further!" He grinned. "I have an invitation to speak before the International Toymakers Council in Brussels. I will ask their members to join us in the boycott so that Santa never leaves the North Pole on Christmas!"

"Brilliant," the president exclaimed.

"A stroke of genius," echoed another TRAA official. With accolades ringing in his ears, the senator turned and waved as he boarded his plane.

Santa's future was now in doubt, not only in America but perhaps also throughout the world.

Chapter 4

Growing Up with the Greedy McGreedy

Travis McGreedy's early popularity was questionable, but he possessed a great ego and felt he could do no wrong. Born in the late 1960s, he craved the limelight and would do anything to get attention. He was that way in elementary school.

He was the tallest student in his class. When he reached 8th grade, he stood over six feet tall. Teachers always placed him in back of the class so as not to block the view of other students. The muscular teenager had an unusually long nose, broken by another student during a fight. He sported his crooked nose all through his career, making him easily identifiable in political cartoons.

There was always a restlessness within McGreedy, and he would vent his frustration on others, frequently staring them down with his deep-set, dark brown eyes. He often bullied his classmates especially the ones he sensed didn't appreciate him.

His father, George, worked as a salesman in a small neighborhood retail store. The McGreedy family, compared to others in the community, appeared to live beyond their means, driving a new car every year and wearing what appeared to be designer clothes.

George was fired from his job two days before Christmas Eve, despite the fact he had been the store's top salesman for almost ten years. He had been caught stealing items and making huge profits by selling them to friends. Young Travis wasn't aware of the circumstance, but he never forgave the store's management for terminating his father during the holiday season.

In the years that followed, Travis's father moved from job to job. Money was scarce. His mother, Alberta, had taken ill and was no longer able to work as a housemaid. There were few gifts for Travis.

As Christmas presents grew scarce, Travis grew more bitter. He told friends he didn't believe in Santa Claus and rejected any sympathy shown by his friends. Truth told, he now hated the Santa he had once revered as a child.

Take nothing away from McGreedy, who was not brilliant but cunning. And so it was that he met Sally Shepherd during his freshman year in a small college in the state of Utah. Sally was the brains behind McGreedy, who was always attending political rallies on campus. She did his homework.

McGreedy became known for voicing his displeasure on most issues. He chided elected county and state politicians and even went so far as to challenge Presidents of the United States.

At age 28, Travis McGreedy and Sally decided that his future was in government. He joined a small, fledgling political organization called the New Party, whose leader was just as radical as Travis. His aim was to replace local and national public servants with people who had dubious reputations, like himself.

Along the way, McGreedy married Sally. Their two sons were told not to believe in Santa Claus and that he was only a myth. Travis went on to become a leader of the New Party who was elected an alderman in his town. He later became mayor, was elected to the House of Representatives in 2012 and finally to the Senate in 2016, along with a majority of New Party members.

By this time he was approaching 60 and had a following of political misfits. Among them were Senators William Whimpers, Jake Taker, Morton Trublood, now President of the United States, and Representative Susan Simpler, a real estate auctioneer who became the Speaker of the House of Representatives. Travis got them elected, and they knew they owed him.

Before ever seeking a political office, Trublood was a farmer in Michigan and often spoke on behalf of other farmers at town hall meetings. It was those eloquent speeches that earned him election as his

The Santa Claus Trial

Travis McGreedy

town's mayor, followed by a seat in the House of Representatives, where his record was unimpressive. And now he was President.

Though many good senators seemed certain to vote against the self-serving bill drafted by McGreedy and his staff, there do not seem to be enough to stop the Senate from passing the Santa Tariff Act, which is at the top of McGreedy's agenda. As he expected, the House has already given its approval to the bill.

Chapter 5

Santa Receives a Subpoena

Now that the House of Representatives had easily passed the Santa Tariff Act, it moved to the Senate Finance Committee where Senator McGreedy was poised to begin his campaign to embarrass and keep Santa Claus from bringing his toys to American children.

Nevertheless, public outcry demanded an explanation. In an attempt to quell mounting opposition, McGreedy decided to hold a special hearing on December 23, the day before the bill was to be brought to the Senate chamber for a final vote.

McGreedy's senior aide flew to the North Pole and delivered a subpoena, a legal document requiring Santa to testify before a special subcommittee of the U.S. Committee on Commerce in Washington, D.C., on December 23rd.

But there was a problem: Santa was not an American citizen; he resided in a section of the frigid North Pole where no country claimed territorial rights. He was not obligated to attend the hearings and indicated that he would not.

Should that be the case, McGreedy could

Santa receives a subpoena.

consider Santa's absence a victory. After all, who could say he did not try to be a fair public servant? McGreedy would have no problem in quickly passing the tariff bill in a Senate where his New Party was in the majority.

A subcommittee was to consist of fourteen senators, eight representing the New Party and two each from the Democrat, Republican, and Independent parties. California Senator Georgie Ann Gruff of the New Party would be the only woman on the panel. Before moving on to the Senate, she was a massage therapist chosen by McGreedy to successfully run as a Congresswoman in 2012, the year he began building his dynasty.

In his *Daily Sunlight* columns, Camper continued to hammer away at McGreedy and his New Party, calling them "a gang of unqualified misfits" and the upcoming hearing a joke. He asked how the New Party could suddenly disregard a Christmas tradition that began hundreds of years ago and became enduringly popular in the United States and Canada during the 20th century.

"What will we tell our children on Christmas morning … that our country has turned on Santa Claus?" he wrote. "What will they think of us?"

He wrote that President Trublood was the nation's best hope. He could veto the Santa Tariff Act, which would put an end to all this nonsense. But

Trublood was a New Party politician who was beholden to McGreedy for the post he now enjoyed, Camper wrote. It would take a miracle for him to veto the bill.

New York Senator Josh Rightman was chosen to speak for the minority lawmakers. Camper called him the panel's "only shining light." Rightman was highly regarded for championing civil rights, freedom of speech (the First Amendment), and listening to the people in his constituency.

But could Rightman outmaneuver McGreedy and convince many New Party lawmakers to change their votes? Unless he can, Santa's visit to America's homes on Christmas Eve will never happen.

Chapter 6

Camper Visits Senator Rightman

Camper paid a visit to Senator Rightman's office on Capitol Hill. The men shook hands and started with small talk. "Heard your granddaughter has been admitted to Columbia University, Senator," Camper said. "Congratulations!"

"Yes, we're very proud of young Zoey's academic accomplishments," the senator replied. "What's happening with Sara and Brandon?" he asked.

"Well, in a way, that's why I'm here," Camper replied. "They know what Senator McGreedy is attempting to do and are not happy Campers. Brandon and Sara have started a letter-writing campaign with students in their school to President Trublood, asking him to prevent this hearing from happening and to veto the bill if it's passed by the Senate."

"The President vetoing the bill? That's unlikely; he's too weak of a man," retorted 58-year-old Rightman. "He belongs to McGreedy. And guess who's calling all the shots? Let's face it, McGreedy is a nightmare who should never have been elected."

"We realize that now," Camper added. "The

New Party would have never gotten a foothold in Congress if it were not for the poor shape of our economy. Parents still find it difficult to adequately feed their families, and millions of the homeless and jobless can be found in long lines waiting to enjoy free meals at soup kitchens. Not good."

After a slight pause, Camper finally asked the big question. "Can you do anything to stop this mindless tragedy from happening?"

Rightman walked behind his desk, sat down, and leaned forward in his chair. "Bill it's a good bet the vote will be very close. I will give it my best shot and hope they will listen to me. There is no doubt we have the support of the majority of the people- not only in the United States- but throughout the world. The best testimonial is the millions of letters and tweets we continue to receive from people opposed to the proposed bill."

He continued, "Bill, did you ever get the name of the man who called you recently, alleging he had evidence that Senator McGreedy was unlawfully taking money and gifts from the Toymakers and Retailers Association of America's board of directors?"

"No," Camper said, "he won't identify himself, although he said he had a video that would show McGreedy was not acting in the interest of our country. Said he would get back to me. We're unable

The Santa Claus Trial

"Can you do anything to stop this
mindless tragedy from happening?"

to prove the senator is misleading the nation unless we have the proof in our hands. And that might be all that we need to derail the Santa bill."

Camper walked toward the door, turned, and waved good bye.

He wondered how successful Senator Rightman can be in convincing New Party senators to forgo the tariff. Will the mysterious caller contact Camper once again? People around the world are sure to be glued to their television sets if Santa makes his appearance before the Senate subcommittee on December 23rd.

As soon as Camper returned to the editorial offices of the *Daily Sunlight*, he succeeded in placing a call to Santa, who was in his workshop supervising elves that were making thousands of toys for deserving children throughout the world.

He identified himself as a reporter and asked if he might be able to discuss the tariff with him personally. After some hesitation, Santa agreed to the meeting, providing that Camper could get to the North Pole.

Camper's next hurdle would be his managing editor, who would have to agree to pay expenses for the flight. With newspaper advertising revenues down, that would not be an easy task.

Camper had time to sit down and start writing a column about the conversation he had had with Senator Rightman, whom he described as a courageous public servant. He urged the public to rally behind "this great American." His article would appear on the front page of the newspaper's morning edition, on its Web site, and in the 82 other newspapers that carried Camper's column.

The hearing and debate were now just two days away, and the world eagerly awaited the outcome.

Chapter 7

The Santa Claus Conspiracy

Senator McGreedy is taking no chances in losing his confrontation with Santa Claus at the hearing, which is scheduled for December 23. Should Santa show up, McGreedy will use the occasion as an opportunity to paint a picture of the generous old man as a selfish person who doesn't want to provide the funding that McGreedy contends the nation desperately needs.

He called a meeting for some of his New Party members at his office in Washington to make sure they understood that Santa must not win any points, especially since the hearing will be televised throughout the world and covered by a pack of journalists. He also expressed concern about the hostile reaction he and the Party may get from the crowd sitting in the gallery above the Senate floor.

The conniving senator realizes he faces humiliation if Santa disregards the bill after it is approved by the Senate, later signed by the President and becomes the law. What if Santa decides to fly to America's homes anyhow on Christmas Eve? He would have the support of the American public and his defiant move might lead to a political disaster for the New Party.

McGreedy, true to form, has a plan to share with his malcontent brethren this morning. A few of the lawmakers attending this session will take their place on the Senate subcommittee in an attempt to make Santa look foolish.

Those present are not the brightest people on this planet, including Senators Harold Hardknocks and Charles Cantdo who have reasonable records but decided to switch to the New Party when it was obvious it was going to win the 2016 election.

McGreedy sat at the center of the round table in the center of his office and was the first to speak. "Glad you all were able to attend this important meeting. How many of you are suspicious of Santa Claus?"

"I think he's a Communist," said Senator Thomas Taker, once a blackjack dealer in Las Vegas.

"Good answer, Senator, but why do you think he's a Communist?," asked McGreedy.

"Because he wears red clothes!" the dealer shot back.

"How about his white beard? I think it's fake and, if it isn't, he ought to shave it off," Senator Georgie Ann Gruff said. "Disgusting!"

"Excellent observation, Annie. Makes a lot of sense. However, let's get down to some serious business. Everyone here knows how important it is to get the votes required to approve the Santa Tariff Act, which was passed on to us by the House of Representatives," McGreedy continued. "The Democrats, Republicans and Independent will attempt to defeat our bill. We cannot let that happen!

"We must fight fire with fire, and I expect each and every one of you to take to the floor and defend our bill." He paused and looked around.

"After all, you are looked upon by many members in Congress as leaders of our Party. No doubt, the biggest challenge to the bill will come from Senate Minority Leader Josh Rightman. We have to stifle him!"

It was Hardknocks' turn. "Let's face it, Travis. This is not a popular move by our Party. I'm tired of the thousands of phone calls reaching my office every day ... the avalanche of outrage on Twitter and Facebook and YouTube. Perhaps we ought to think this over before calling for a vote."

"I'm surprised by your remark," sneered McGreedy. "You, of all people, one of the mainstays of our Party. Remember, Harold, politics is not for the weary."

"You know, Travis, he has a point," Cantdo said. "Santa is a living legend. How are we going to defend

The Santa Claus Trial

"Glad you all were able to attend
this important meeting...."

our action—and what is the world going to think of us?"

McGreedy seemed to have expected some opposition and responded with withering sarcasm. "I realize that both you and Harold once belonged to the opposition before you abandoned your respective parties three years ago to join our winning team. Yes, I'm sorry to hear you are no longer friends with Senator Rightman. Nevertheless, Charlie ... Harold, ... you must follow our Party's wishes at all times. I hope I've made myself very clear."

"Indeed you've made yourself very clear," Hardknocks replied sarcastically. "So I ask, considering the bad press we have been getting, especially from reporter Bill Camper, how are we going to justify passing the Santa Tariff Act?"

"Camper can write as many articles as he wants to, but it won't do him any good," McGreedy said.

Georgie Ann Gruff appeared to be puzzled by McGreedy's comment. "I'm not sure what you mean," she said.

"We're listening," said House Speaker Susan Simpler as she continued to knit a sweater, vigorously chew her gum and occasionally blow bubbles.

Slowly and deliberately, McGreedy began to reveal his strategy.

"Yesterday, one of my senior aides flew to the North Pole and presented a subpoena to Mr. Claus. I would have given a hundred dollars to watch the expression on his face," McGreedy said with a laugh.

"Where would you get the money, Travis? The Treasury? It's broke," said Deputy Chief of Staff Mitch Mouthwater, a Southern gentleman and former used-car dealer who first met McGreedy at a New Party convention in Memphis, TN in 2012 and had been his confidante since.

Not pleased, McGreedy retorted, "Very funny, Mouthwater."

"Why the subpoena?" asked Georgie Ann Gruff. "I don't get it. Everyone knows Mr. Claus is not a citizen of the United States and is not bound by it."

"Strategy, my friends......strategy," McGreedy said slyly. "If Mr. Claus agrees to come to Washington—and my guess is he will—and pay $1.00 for each of his gifts, we could cut the national deficit by trillions of dollars and our New Party could once again become the shining light on the Hill."

"What makes you so sure Mr. Claus has the wherewithal to pay trillions of dollars?" asked Vice President Brad Bragger, who will be presiding over the hearing. Although serving one term as a senator, his good looks and smooth oratory helped attract women voters during the crucial election in 2016 won by the New Party.

McGreedy grinned. "Well, he's got the magic corn that enables his reindeer to fly. The man is a magician. He should be able to come up with the money."

Senator Walter Whimpers, formerly a sanitation inspector in Ames, Iowa, who ran on a promise to "clean things up," timidly entered the discussion. "What if he refuses to come to Washington?"

"By refusing to testify, he is not only defying the subpoena but telling America's children he doesn't care. In that case, he will not be permitted to fly over our country," explained McGreedy.

"Oh, my. And what happens if he decides to fly to our homes on Christmas Eve?" inquired Whimpers.

Not inclined to stop her knitting, Susan Simpler shouted, "Shoot him down!" That was the plan McGreedy had secretly discussed with her prior to the meeting.

Except for Hardknocks and Cantdo, everyone applauded.

"I think that's possible," McGreedy answered.

"Stop there!" demanded Hardknocks. "If you shoot Santa down, the whole world will never forgive you. You've got to be crazy!"

McGreedy continued to unveil his plan, by now on a rant. "What if our Intelligence found out that Santa was going to seek revenge after we pass the bill and, soon afterward, learned he was going to fly over Washington with a nuclear bomb? Eh?"

He leaned forward in his chair. "If that's true, and there's no reason to believe otherwise, President Trublood would give the order to shoot him down and...and the entire world will praise our government for its quick action." McGreedy caught his breath.

"Surely children everywhere will miss Santa's Christmas Eve flyovers, but they will understand America had to defend itself."

Not a sound was heard. Finally, Cantdo broke the silence. "Travis, I don't think we have to resort to killing Santa Claus," he began. "After all, he may not decide to defy our government. There is an easier way to stop him from delivering those toys to our children."

"And may I ask what your great idea is?" a combative McGreedy challenged.

"Let Congress pass a law making it mandatory for all homeowners to place lids on their chimneys."

"Won't work," Mouthwater interjected.

"Why not?" Cantdo asked.

"Ya'll should know there's not enough time to pass such a law, and it would take weeks before the public could act," Mouthwater said. "Sorry, Senator".

"Enough!" McGreedy barked. "Some of you will join others on the subcommittee. I will be the chairman."

"Suh, you are the Senate Majority Leader and shouldn't be chairman of this committee," Mouthwater noted.

"Mitch, I'll discuss that issue with you later. Meeting adjourned."

Chapter 8

Camper Seeks Funding for Trip to North Pole

Camper was still writing his column about Rightman and the Santa crisis when he decided to take a coffee break and strode toward the vending machine located in the hallway outside the newsroom. His reputation for supporting Santa and columns criticizing Senator McGreedy and his New Party hadn't gone unnoticed by his fellow journalists.

"Hey, Santa, how we doing?" joked one of his buddies as Camper passed his desk.

Another, investigative reporter Art Snider, walked up to him and shook his hand. "Bill, all of us are behind you. Good job. Don't stop; keep it going. McGreedy deserves to be impeached."

"Thanks, my friend," Camper replied. "We've just begun to fight back. Besides, I'm heading to Stuffy's office to get his blessings."

"For what?"

"I need to fly to the North Pole tomorrow, interview Santa and bring him back with me to

Washington for the Senate hearing the next day."

"Are you kidding? A stupendous idea! What a scoop that would be! Go for it!"

"Just got one obstacle," Camper said. "The 'old man'." The two reporters nodded as they referred to Managing Editor Albert "Stuffy" Levine. "He's told us countless times that we all have to be cost-effective."

"You're right," Snider said. "We've already lost nine reporters because our advertising revenues have slumped."

"Yeah, I know. But there's always hope," Camper said as he marched toward Stuffy's office.

"Good luck," shouted Snider. "You'll need it. Stuffy isn't a pushover."

Camper kept moving forward. "I realize that!"

He stopped in front of Stuffy's glass office door and could see him sitting behind his desk that was piled high with various editions of the newspaper. As usual, Stuffy chewed on an unlit cigar. He waved Camper in.

Stuffy was the recipient of many journalism awards during his forty years as a reporter and editor. He was given his nickname by fellow reporters who covered the police beat with him in his younger days, where many journalists traditionally start their careers reporting on crime, accidents, or other local stories from the city's police stations.

The Santa Claus Trial

"What do you want now?"

The Santa Claus Trial

During lunch or dinner breaks, Levine would display an extraordinary fondness for food, almost stuffing himself and then washing everything down with a beer or two. That habit and the nickname also applied to the pouch-like belly now carried around by this 64-year-old short, balding man who had been promoted to his present post a decade earlier.

"What do you want now?" asked Levine with a smile. "I told you I can't give you a raise until we get more advertising dollars," he teased.

"I know, Stuffy. That's not the reason I'm here."

"Really? What a surprise. Speak up."

"Well, I want to go to the North Pole tomorrow, interview Santa, and bring him back to Washington for the Senate hearing on the 23rd. Want to know how he thinks and what he feels about testifying at the hearing. I want to see his workshop and talk to his elves, find out why he can't afford to pay the tariff. I want to tell his story not only to Americans, but to the world. I'm sure he'll be okay with that."

Stuffy Levine listened intently as Camper continued.

"Besides, I got a tip from a caller who gave me some inside information about the senator. He's told me something I've always suspected, that McGreedy's trying to sell the American public on the fact that the tax on Santa is needed to help our nation's struggling economy.

"But the truth is that he's made a secret pact with the Toymakers and Retailers Association of America. The organization represents manufacturers and retailers who see themselves making more profit if they can eliminate the competition from Santa Claus."

Stuffy held up one hand and signaled Camper to stop. "Follow through on the informant and ask him if he will be willing to go on record. As for your trip to the North Pole, though, it's not in my budget. And you say the hearing's on the 23rd? That's the day after tomorrow!"

"*Hearing?*" Camper nearly shouted. "You've got to be kidding! It's a trial! Senator McGreedy is the prosecutor, and members of the New Party will be the jury. Santa is the lone defendant and will not be successful in proving his case. The cards are stacked against him! It's a 100-to-1 shot the Santa Tariff Act will pass the Senate the next day and be signed by our spineless President. This so-called hearing is a joke on the American people!"

"Bill, I understand where you're coming from, but ..."

"Aw, c'mon Stuffy," interrupted Camper. "I have a friend who was a pilot in the Iraq war. He buys and sells old planes. I'm confident I can count on him to rent and pilot the plane for very little money. And you won't have to pay for our meals."

"What do you mean, I won't have to pay for

your meals?"

"Kate and I will pack lunches and dinners. I love sandwiches! And you love scoops like this!"

Stuffy scratched his head. "I- I - don't know. Let me think about it."

"C'mon, have a heart, Stuffy."

"You know, it's a coincidence that our Jewish Hanukkah holiday and Christmas usually fall on almost the same December dates," Stuffy reflected. "But, with all due respect, Bill, my children and grandchildren don't expect a visit from Santa Claus on Christmas Eve. Instead, they will be playing games commemorating rededication of the Temple in Jerusalem and defeat of the Syrian army in 165 A.D."

"Stuffy, rightfully, to each his own," said Camper as he leaned on the edge of his boss' desk. "Granted, Christmas is a Christian holiday, but I'll bet you a box of cigars that even though your youngsters don't believe that Santa Claus lives, they probably enjoy reading stories about him and his reindeer.

"Anyhow, aside from Hanukkah, our paper has published features every year on the celebration of other gift-giving, multicultural holidays like Kwanzaa, Diwali, and Ramadan. Almost all of those American children do believe in Santa Claus and are expecting to open Santa's gifts Christmas morning." Camper took a deep breath and continued.

"But that's not going to happen unless we build a greater awareness of what Senator McGreedy is really up to and gain wider support from the public. I want to write my interview with Santa so it appears the day before the Senate hearing. That's just three days from now. It's wake-up time, Stuffy!"

"How are you going to get in to see the bearded wonder who keeps people away from his property at the northernmost end of the Earth?" Levine asked.

"He's agreed to an interview. This is too important an issue for him to deny me a visit. Trust me."

"All right, I'm convinced," the managing editor said. "You'll get a limited expense account that should cover the fuel required for the trip and light meals for you and the pilot at refueling stops. Get some photos and come back and give our newspaper a story that deserves a Pulitzer Prize."

Stuffy picked up the inter-office phone to speak to his accountant. "Mary, I'm sending Camper to your office. He's going to need some money for a trip to the North Pole. He'll see you in a few minutes."

Camper would soon be on his way to visit Santa.

Chapter 9

The Flight to the North Pole

Camper arrived at a small airport outside the city limits on the morning of December 21st, where he was reunited with Rickey Rodriguez, a former helicopter pilot he had met while reporting on the war in Iraq. They had been corresponding with one another ever since Rickey's discharge from the Army in 2008.

Rodriguez, a collector of vintage planes, had immediately agreed to accept the challenge presented by Camper. He chose to use his own renovated Beech 18 plane for the trip. The twin-engine plane, which saw military service during and after World War II, normally seats two in the cockpit and five in the cabin. This time it would only be carrying three passengers.

At the last minute Camper had decided to take his 11-year-old son, Brandon, with him on the trip to the North Pole. Brandon had pleaded with his father to tag along since he and other students were enjoying their holiday reprieve from school. Sara had also asked to come along, but there were weight limitations due to the fact that Rodriguez had installed and filled additional fuel tanks on the plane.

The Santa Claus Trial

"I'm about to meet the real
Santa Claus. Awesome!"

Bill and Brandon carried the food, camera equipment, and other supplies aboard, while Rodriguez checked the plane's instruments, engines, tires, and fuel tanks. He told Camper everything was in order and placed on his headphones to receive directions for takeoff from the controller in the airport tower. He had filed a flight plan and would continue to communicate with air controllers along the way. Camper crawled into the cockpit seat alongside Rodriquez as he started the engines. Brandon strapped himself into a single seat behind them. They were on their way to visit Santa.

The takeoff was smooth, and the plane climbed to a comfortable altitude on this cloudless day, winging its way to the North Pole. The flight took them over Canada and to Anchorage, Alaska, both places targeted for refueling stops. The farther north they flew, the colder and darker it became.

Brandon kept himself busy during the long journey, listening to music on his iPod, reading books, and occasionally looking out of the plane's windows, curious as to what the landscape below looked like. He was awed by the sight of the seemingly never-ending pristine snow.

There were meal breaks in the plane. Brandon and his father munched on peanut butter and jelly sandwiches during lunch and turkey sandwiches at dinner. Rodriquez preferred different varieties of tacos prepared and packed by his wife.

It was nearing midnight as they left Anchorage on the last leg of their flight. They were rapidly approaching Santa's home and a small lighted airstrip situated on the thick ice of the Arctic Ocean. They would be landing in the dark. The sun is above the horizon at the North Pole during the summer months and is below the horizon in the winter months, when temperatures average about 32 degrees below zero.

"I can see the red and blue lights on Santa's runway!" Rodriguez reported.

"Wow!" exclaimed Brandon as he rushed to the cockpit and patted his father on the shoulder. "I can't believe it! I can hardly wait to tell Mom and Sara and my buddies that I'm about to meet the real Santa Claus. Awesome!"

"Calm down," Camper said firmly. "Get back in your seat and refasten your seat belt. We're going in for a tricky landing."

Rodriguez began communicating with a controller in the tower managed by Santa's elves. "This is the plane carrying Bill Camper," he told them.

"I hear you, Beech 18. Santa is expecting him," a voice replied. "Approach the runway from the north, where the visibility is clearer."

"10-4. Coming in!"

Rodriguez made a smooth landing on the icy runway, although there were some anxious moments as the plane skidded toward the tower before finally stopping, with the engines cooling down. Camper drew a deep breath.

"Whew, that was close!" he said. "Guess we're all tired. We'll clean up the plane tomorrow. Get your winter gear and backpacks ready. Santa's waiting to see us!"

A huge sleigh drawn by four reindeer stopped alongside the plane. It was driven by a lone elf in a red suit covered by a green winter jacket. His pointy ears and long nose caused Brandon to nudge his father and whisper in his ear, "Dad, he's one of Santa's helpers."

"But of course," Camper answered. "They're his work force and make the toys that are delivered to children throughout the world on Christmas Eve. Your friends may not be so lucky if Senator McGreedy gets his way."

"Mr. and Mrs. Claus are eager to meet you," the elf shouted as he tried to compete with the sound of the plane's engines, which were winding down. "Who's the youngster with you?"

"He's my son, Brandon," Bill shouted back.

"Boy, is he going to have fun! Hop aboard!"

The sleigh passed a large gate, where the subpoena had been dropped off, and stopped in front of Santa's two-story, unpretentious red brick house. Visits to his property were restricted. The Campers and Rodriguez had the privilege of becoming the first persons ever to see what his home really looked like.

They were greeted at the front door by the short, plump, jolly old white-bearded man himself. He was wearing dark blue jeans held up by wide white suspenders over an open-collared red shirt. "Mrs. Claus and I are delighted you all arrived safely. Please come in."

Camper, Rodriguez, and Brandon hesitated as they entered the house. Brandon, who had visualized Santa's physical stature greater than it was, tapped his father on the back and whispered with astonishment into Camper's ear. "Dad, I'm almost as tall as Santa."

"No, son, not really; you still have a ways to go."

The three took off their jackets and handed them to an elf named Horatio. Mrs. Claus entered the comfortably furnished living room carrying cups of steaming hot chocolate on a tray. She was wearing a pink blouse and a long blue skirt covered by a white apron. Her white hair was neatly combed into a bun. Meanwhile, Santa sat down in his rocking chair and reached for his long-stemmed pipe.

"Cold out there," said Mrs. Claus as she handed each a cup. "Please move to our fireplace, where you can get warm. Afterward, Horatio can show you your rooms, where you can wash up before we serve dinner."

"Thank you, ma'am," replied a grateful

Rodriguez. Shortly afterward, the trio was directed to their rooms.

It wasn't long before they sat down for a candlelight dinner consisting of cooked ham, mashed potatoes, peas, and pumpkin pie for dessert. Near the end of the meal Brandon broke the silence. "Thanks, Mr. and Mrs. Claus! This beats the sandwiches Mom and Dad made."

"Ho, Ho, Ho," laughed Santa. "You're welcome Brandon. It's getting late and I'm sure all of you are tired from that long plane ride. Bill, before we sit down and talk tomorrow, I'll take all of you on a morning tour of the property and our workshop. Until then," he said, "let's make a toast."

They lifted their water glasses and Santa smiled as he said, "Merry Christmas, or shall we say Feliz Navidad, Mr. Rodriguez?"

Note: Flight and airplane data provided by Taigh Rame of Vintage Aircraft in Stockton, CA 95206.

Chapter 10

Getting Ready

It was early morning when Camper awoke. He saw that Brandon was still asleep in the other bed. "C'mon, sleepy head," he said as he gently shook him. "Breakfast is waiting and Santa is going to give us a tour of his workshop."

Brandon rubbed his eyes, yawned, and jumped out of his bed. Both showered and walked to the breakfast table. Rodriguez was the early bird, already feasting on pancakes and strips of bacon when they arrived. "You beat us to it," Bill said. "Did you get enough sleep?"

"Yep, even went to the plane to check the equipment and the tanks. Looks like everything is all right, though we'll have to stop in Anchorage once again for refueling."

"You're the boss, Rickey. Sounds good! Where's Santa?" inquired Camper of Mrs. Claus as she handed red and green colored napkins to each.

"He had his breakfast earlier and is getting the sleigh readied for the trip to our workshop. Should be here soon, so sit down and enjoy your breakfast. Coffee is for the adults, and Brandon, you get plenty

The Santa Claus Trial

"…. sit down and enjoy your breakfast"

of hot chocolate."

An hour passed before Santa made his entrance. "Sorry I'm late," he grunted. "Had to feed the reindeer who will be pulling our sleigh. They have to have their breakfasts too. Ho, Ho, Ho! Well, best we get going. Is everybody ready?"

"You bet," said Camper as he zippered his warm down jacket. "Let's get going. Read a lot about your workshop. We can't wait to see it!"

And out the door they went.

Chapter 11

Santa Gives a Tour of His Workshop

The Campers and Rodriguez hopped aboard the sleigh wearing their winter coats, heavy ski gloves, and hats. Santa covered their laps with a thick blanket before taking the reins. The temperature, as expected, was way below zero, and you could see plumes of hot breath bellowing from their mouths as they conversed with one another during the ride that took them across miles of sparkling snow and thick ice.

"Look!" exclaimed Brandon, his eyes fixed on a lone polar bear in the distance. "Cool!" He reached into his pocket for his camera and took a picture. "Son, you can truly tell your friends that you 'shot' a bear," teased Camper. His comment drew laughter from Rickey and Santa.

"Brandon, it's unusual for us to see animals on this northern section of the Arctic," Santa said. "That bear may be lost. I just don't know. Bears feed on food from the Arctic Ocean and don't find hunting here to their liking. Although once in a great moon we sight a small, white Arctic fox or wild reindeer. Their bodies

The Santa Claus Trial

"Bill, don't forget to mention I'm an Equal Opportunity Employer."

can survive these cold temperatures."

Brandon was silent. Accompanying his father to the North Pole, meeting Mr. and Mrs. Claus, sighting a polar bear, and shortly touring Santa's workshop was awesome.

The sleigh halted before a one-story red concrete building that looked like a great big industrial warehouse. A sign posted over the entrance simply read: *Santa's Workshop*.

They could hear the noises of hammers and drills as they entered the building, the elves were busy at work because it was only two days before Santa would have to pack his sleigh with presents for children living in countries almost everywhere- perhaps the exception being the United States.

Santa acted as the guide during the walk-through and explained that the modern workshop was designed so that elves had their own private sections separated by 12-foot walls. Signs on the doors of each department read: *Electronics, Small Toys, Large Toys, Doll Houses,* and so forth. Storage facilities for the variety of gifts were situated in huge rooms located at the rear of the building, not too far from a dozen or so shipping docks.

The bundled gifts would be loaded onto Santa's stately decorated sleigh with small bells fixed to the harness straps of the reindeer. The bundles were marked for world-wide destinations on Christmas Eve.

"We make different products in each of our departments," Santa explained as they looked to the left and right of the aisles. Elves could be seen busily making either dolls or toy houses, putting together bicycles, computers, and iPods, among other items. The finished products were put on a conveyor belt where they passed under the watchful eyes of quality-control elves who Santa explained must approve each gift before wrapping the presents and storing them in the back rooms.

"Aren't many toys and computers manufactured by companies elsewhere?" Camper asked.

"Yes," Santa began, "but many U.S. companies have given us the rights to build their products, and our engineers frequently improve upon them. You can see that our designer toys are appealing and very unique," he said as he stopped and picked up a smartly decorated toy doll that was not sold in any stores.

As they approached the conveyor belt, Rodriquez noticed a female elf inspecting the toys. He tapped Santa on the shoulder, wondering if his eyes had deceived him. "Santa," he said, "I didn't think there were women elven working here ... only male elves."

"Oh, I see you spotted Rosie. She's one of our many elves."

"Bill," he said with a whimsical smile, "don't forget to mention that I'm an Equal Opportunity

Employer when you write your column."

Camper did manage to interview several of the elves before the tour ended around noon. Santa suggested they return to his home for lunch and then rest. Shortly afterward, he would meet with Camper and decide whether to obey McGreedy's subpoena to testify at tomorrow's Senate hearing.

Chapter 12

A Conversation with Santa

Camper and Santa moved to the den after lunch for the interview. Santa sat on his rocking chair and continuously stroked his white beard as he thoughtfully answered numerous questions and posed for pictures taken periodically by Camper, who sat opposite him.

Most of the questions centered on Santa's possible trip to Washington. It was evident—despite all the prodding by Camper—that he was reluctant to make the trip. The interview and photos would be published in the *Daily Sunlight* and seen on the Internet the following day.

It was late afternoon when the session ended and Santa had finally agreed to appear before the Senate. He would board the twin-engine plane for the flight in a few hours.

But now it was time for him to walk to the stable nearby and check on his eight—make that nine, with Rudolph—trusted reindeer who take him to the rooftops of homes throughout the world Christmas Eve.

Camper took to his laptop to write about his

exclusive interview and Santa's arrival in Washington. Stuffy waited patiently in his office for the story and pictures.

Meanwhile, Brandon's curiosity was at work. He wanted to see the legendary reindeer and received permission to do so. The boy ran to the stable and stood at its entrance until he was noticed by Santa.

"Well, well," said Santa as he stopped brushing the sturdy body of one of his reindeer. "Come in, son, it's a pleasant surprise. I don't think Donner (sometimes referred to as Donder) will mind if I take a break. I suppose you wanted to meet the reindeer that will be flying me around the world on Christmas Eve?"

"Sure do."

Santa took Brandon by the hand and walked around the stable, introducing him to Dasher, Dancer, Prancer, Vixen, Comet, Cupid, and Blitzen. Brandon chuckled as he pointed in the direction of the last and most popular reindeer. "That's got to be Rudolph," Brandon said. "I can tell by his red nose."

"It does glow, doesn't it? He's our leader: We depend on that handsome nose to show us the way, especially in bad weather. Time to feed the reindeer before we leave. Would you like to help me?"

"Yes, sir."

Santa gave Brandon a pail filled with oats and magic corn and helped him carry it as they poured small amounts into each of the deer's feedbag. When they finished, Brandon sat on the straw-covered floor and folded his legs. "Do you mind if I ask a few questions?"

"Not a problem," replied Santa as he sat on his stool peeling a potato he had gotten from a sack alongside of him. "Orders from Mrs. Claus," he said with a smile. "She always makes a great meal for me before I hop on my sled and visit the hundreds of millions of homes—or, I guess, take off in your airplane. What's your question?"

"How many countries do you visit on Christmas Eve?"

"My gosh, a lot! When we leave here we will fly to Newfoundland, Russia, Germany, the Netherlands, Germany, Finland, Canada, and even to the homes of Christian families in the Middle East. Sometimes I think the list is never-ending."

"Will you come to my house in Chicago?"

"I hope so. But it all depends if your people in Congress allow me to deliver my presents in the United States. Right now, it doesn't look good. I just can't afford to pay the taxes they insist upon."

"My father and I will pray for you. So will Mr. Rodriguez."

"You're a wonderful young man," said Santa as he playfully rumpled Brandon's hair. "Any other questions?"

"Yes, my friend's name is Muhammad, and he's a Muslim. He says his family doesn't celebrate Christmas. Can you leave some extra toys for me? I'll give them to him!"

"I don't see why not. Muslims living in many countries may not observe the holiday like Muhammad's family, but some will visit others that do and respectfully exchange gifts. I know that's true in sections of Lebanon."

"How many letters do you get from children every year?"

"Millions, according to records we receive from the main post office in Lapland."

"Can I read some of them?"

"You will find some mailbags stacked right here," and Santa pointed to a large heap of canvas bags. "Help yourself to a few!"

Brandon ran to the bags and came back with a handful of envelopes. The return addresses indicated they were mailed from different countries. "Santa, guess you haven't had a chance to read all of these."

"No, I haven't, although I try to reply to boys and girls your age and younger. Many letters are written with the help of parents and are easier to read. My elves screen all the letters and make sure only those who have been good all year long get presents."

The Santa Claus Trial

'Time to feed the reindeer before we leave."

The Santa Claus Trial

"How do they know who's good and who's bad?"

Santa placed his finger to his mouth as he gave Brandon his familiar wink. "Shhh! Now, that's a secret."

"Oh, well, can I read some of these letters to you?"

"Please do."

Brandon tore open the first envelope and read aloud several of the letters:

"Dear Santa,

My mommy wants to know what kind of cookies you want to eat when you come to our house. She also wants to know if you like skim milk. She tells me she loves you and thinks you should lose a few pounds. P.S. They are diet cookies. Love,

Lisa, 10

Charlotte, North Carolina"

"Buenos Dias Santa,

My name is Silva and I am 12 years old. I live in Teolocholco, Mexico and still have the gifts you left me last Christmas. Many of my friends don't have toys. Please stop by their homes (see list on back) so they can enjoy the true spirit of Christmas. Muchas gracias!"

"Dear Santa,

Please take care of your reindeer on Christmas Eve. My favorite reindeer is Rudolph. I wish you a safe trip.

Susan, 10

Seattle, Washington"

"Dear Mr. Claus,

I am a school teacher in Iraq. Last year, my son Ammar lost his right leg when our church was bombed by some people who don't believe religious families like ours should have attended Midnight Mass. I realize you can't give him his leg back, but the biggest gift you can bring to the world on Christmas Eve is Peace. Merry Christmas!

Rukia B."

Brandon had started to read the last of the letters when he suddenly stopped after saying, "Dear Santa." What was the problem? Surely all the letters he read previously were wonderful. However, the expression on his face indicated there was indeed something wrong. He continued to read the letter silently:

"My brother's name is Brandon and he has lots of the presents you left him last year. He does not need more. That's why I am asking you to leave me extra dolls for my dollhouse. I know he will not care. Thanks.

Sara, 7
Chicago"

Chapter 13

Santa Arrives in Washington, D.C.

Santa bordered the plane after saying goodbye to Mrs. Claus and was seated in the cockpit next to Rodriquez. Bill and Brandon were situated in the rear after removing much of the equipment in order to lighten the load.

Rodriquez started the motors and was ready to takeoff when he noticed that Santa appeared nervous. "Santa you don't seem to be relaxed," Rodriguez said. "Is there something wrong?"

"No, Rickey. As you know, I'm used to flying, but this is the first time I've done it in a plane!"

Santa's arrival was certainly the media's biggest story of the day. A huge crowd waited patiently inside and outside Reagan National Airport, while thousands more marched to the Russell Senate Office Building where the hearing was to take place. Many held signs—*We Love You, Santa! McGreedy is Greedy! Don't Take Away Our Santa! All Americans and God Love Santa!*

Mingling with the crowd in front of the building were the Reverend Robert Jordan and a priest named

Father Frank McCloskey. Each had brought members of his respective congregation to protest the action taken by the Senate's New Party. Rev. Jordan wore a black wide-rimmed fedora and heavy black coat to protect him from the punishing wind on this nasty winter morning. Father McCloskey was dressed in a gray winter jacket and was wearing black earmuffs; you could easily recognize his priestly white collar.

They had met while they were serving as chaplains in the Navy and remained in touch after their retirement several years ago. There was no hesitation when Father McCloskey contacted Rev. Jordan and asked him to join him in the protest march.

Father McCloskey's Catholic Church is located in a low-income neighborhood on the outskirts of Washington, D.C.; Rev. Jordan's Baptist church is in a small Mississippi town.

The African American minister had quickly ordered a bus, which he filled with parishioners the night before. They set out and were eager to show their support for Santa upon arriving in Washington, where they were greeted by cold winter temperatures and a whipping wind.

The parishioners ranged from teenagers to older adults, many of whom could be seen tapping their shoes on the cold, hard pavement to keep the circulation in their feet constant. The Rev. Jordan grabbed his bullhorn and told his parishioners they could battle the cold by moving around. "We gotta' keep warm," he shouted loudly. "Ain't nothing like this where we come from," he chuckled.

Meanwhile, the plane continued its flight with a not-so-jolly Santa, who had decided to attend the hearing only after a persuasive argument by Camper.

"You can't disappoint millions of American children who look up to you every Christmas," Camper had told him. "You have to show McGreedy you are not afraid of him. It's showtime, Santa!"

As they got close to the airport, Santa confided, "You know, Bill, I'm not an American citizen. I feel funny testifying before a bunch of politicians I never heard of."

"Santa, on Christmas Eve you're as American as apple pie!" Camper shouted above the engine noise.

Because the plane was behind its scheduled arrival time, an impatient McGreedy had ordered the North American Aerospace Defense Command, stationed in Colorado, to check on its whereabouts. The NAADC is responsible for tracking Santa's Christmas Eve journey around the world.

Within a few minutes after the sighting was reported, the plane approached the airport, escorted by three jet fighters from New Mexico's Holloman Air Force Base.

Beech 18 taxied down the runway and came to a

The Santa Claus Trial

Santa arrives in Washington for the hearing.

halt not too far from the gate where Kate Camper was waiting with several Secret Service agents. She had received her credentials after explaining she was Santa's attorney and would be at his side during this morning's hearings.

The plane's door opened and steps were lowered. Brandon was the first to exit and rushed into his mother's arms. "Mom, it was an awesome trip!"

"We missed you," she said as she kissed him on the forehead. "Where's your father?"

"There he is!" he said pointing to Bill as he stepped down from the plane. He waved back to her. Now it was Santa's turn. The cherubic, white-bearded figure appeared at the door of the plane wearing his red coat with white collar and cuffs, white-cuffed trousers, black leather belt and boots, and red and white cap. His red cheeks were as prominent as his smile.

He waved to the hysterical crowd before being escorted by Bill to where Kate was standing. "Hi, Kate," said Bill as he embraced his wife and kissed her. "Kate, meet Santa Claus!"

"Glad to meet you," said Kate as she shook his hand. "I will be representing you in the hearing."

"It is and will be my pleasure, Mrs. Camper. Shall we get on our way?"

"Yes, our transportation is nearby," replied Kate.

The Santa Claus Trial

The four made their trip to the Russell Senate Office Building in a black stretch limousine driven by a Secret Service agent. Other agents followed in a black SUV.

History was about to be made.

Chapter 14

Santa's Testimony Begins

The limousine pulled up in front of the office building, and the driver got out. He quickly opened the side door, allowing Kate, Bill, and Brandon to step out. They were followed by an unhappy Santa, who found himself facing the flashbulbs of newspaper and magazine photographers, as well as television reporters who were barraging him with questions: *"Do you have the money to pay for the tariff? Are you going to let Senator McGreedy disappoint America's children?"*

Two Secret Service agents led the way as the group entered the rotunda and carefully walked up one of the two marble staircases leading to the entrance of the Kennedy Caucus Room. The chants of protesters could be heard outside. They were shouting in unison: *"Down with McGreedy!"* and *"We love Santa!"*

The room they were about to enter is the site of the Senate's most significant public hearings.

The first hearing occurred there in 1912, shortly after the sinking of the *Titanic* in the Atlantic; another occurred in 1924, when the Senate Banking Committee examined Wall Street banks and the Stock

Exchange. The installation of television cameras later enabled politicians like Senator Joseph McCarthy to use the room to publicize his charges of Communist subversion and espionage in the federal government in the 1950s. The controversial nomination of Supreme Court Justice Clarence Thomas occurred there in 1991.

People could expect the Santa Claus hearing to be among those that would not be soon forgotten.

Kate and Santa entered the room. Santa surveyed its high decorated and gilded ceiling and large crystal chandelier. The three oversized French windows, marble walls, and columns were impressive.

"Don't know why they need my money," Santa laughed.

"Yes, you can be sure our taxes paid for whoever designed this room," Kate replied.

They sat down. A microphone was situated on each side of the table. Both were soon joined by a short, bald-headed man with a neatly trimmed mustache. He was wearing a black pinstriped suit and a black shirt with a red tie. He sat a short distance from Kate and Santa and carried a briefcase, which he hurriedly opened. He reached in and took a small stack of papers from it. Who is he? Kate wondered. And what is he doing here?

Kate's credentials as a lawyer could not be challenged. After graduating from the University of Chicago Law School with high honors, she became a state's attorney and later worked as a federal prosecutor, winning several high-profile cases. She was now a partner at her father's law firm, Doherty & Camper, situated in the city's Near North community.

Kate and Santa could see the fourteen members of the subcommittee seated on a raised platform overlooking the Senate floor. Among the New Party members were Senators Thomas Taker, Walter Whimpers, Henry Henpeck, and Georgie Ann Gruff. Senators Josh Rightman, John Justice, and Harold Henessey were among the minority members.

Unless one of the New Party members should decides to challenge McGreedy and vote for Santa, it is almost certain the bill would be approved by the subcommittee, whose members are in the majority. If that is the case, Minority Leader Rightman will give the rebuttal when the full Senate meets to vote on the bill the following day, December 24th. He hopes to persuade enough New Party members to switch their votes and defeat the Santa Tariff Act.

Camper decided to take Brandon with him up to the gallery, where he could take notes and talk to the men and women who had come to witness the hearings. Later, they would head to the nearby press room, where reporters write their stories on laptops and forward them to their respective newspapers, radio, and television stations. Some use cell phones while others make live reports before TV cameras.

McGreedy made sure he served as chairman of the panel. He stood up, his reading glasses hanging halfway down his crooked nose, pounded the gavel, and announced the start of the hearing. He requested Santa to stand up and raise his right hand.

"That's OK," Kate whispered to a hesitant Santa, who clearly was not used to this type of confrontation. "Go ahead and stand up."

McGreedy asked Santa to take the usual oath given to individuals who testify before the Senate, swearing to tell "the truth, the whole truth, so help him God." He did.

"Please be seated," McGreedy said.

There was a silence as McGreedy fiddled with his microphone and prepared to address Santa. This was his glorious moment and he did not want it to get away without receiving the media coverage he thirsted for. As always, in nationwide events such as this one, he would play to the television cameras and strike poses he knew appealed to newspaper reporters and photographers. He began: "Mr. Santa Claus, this is nothing personal but …"

Before he finished his sentence he heard the boos from people in the gallery.

McGreedy pounded his gavel on the large table once again and threatened the onlookers, telling them they would be removed if there were further outbreaks. But the chance of that happening was slim,

The Santa Claus Trial

inasmuch as McGreedy didn't want to show the world he was a mean old man.

"Now, Mr. Claus ... Is that really your name?"

"Of course," Santa smiled. "Has been for hundreds of years although some people in other countries call me by different names."

"Please explain."

"Well, sir, I am indeed Santa Claus. I hope your eyes don't deceive you." His response drew loud laughter from the gallery. Santa turned to Kate and winked, obviously enjoying some attention himself.

McGreedy was not amused. Once again he used his gavel in an attempt to silence the crowd.

"Go on, Mr. Claus. What do you mean by different names?"

"Well, sir, the Dutch call me Sinter Klaas, the English, Father Christmas, and in France I'm known as Pere Noel."

"How about St. Nicholas?" Senator Whimpers asked.

"And how about Kris Kringle?" Senator Gruff followed.

"Could be. You see, countries have different rituals, traditions, and customs based on their historical roots. But the bottom line, Senators, is that there is only one Santa Claus and he's standing before you...

you nitwits! Ho, ho, ho," he heartily laughed, looking up at the people in the gallery.

Santa's response was greeted by a loud round of applause. "That's telling 'em Santa!" a voice bellowed from the gallery. Another yelled, "Why don't you ask Santa for his birth certificate?"

Kate, surprised by Santa's comment, pleaded for him to be more respectful and to apologize. Meanwhile, McGreedy was busy banging his gavel. "Order! Order! This is the last time I will be tolerating the behavior of you people in the gallery!" He then stared menacingly at Santa.

"You don't seem to show much respect for members of the Senate."

"Well, sir, you don't seem to show much respect for the meaning of Christmas."

McGreedy then began to embark on his insincere speech, posing for the television cameras. "Let me remind you, Mr. Claus, you are here for one reason ... and only one reason ... and that is to help save our great, great country from financial doom. We are not abandoning the Christmas spirit as many may think, simply finding ways and means for our government to obtain additional capital. We can only accomplish our goal if we raise taxes ... anywhere we can. You can help us by, ahem, paying your share.

"Everyone loves you Mr. Claus, as I do," McGreedy continued. "Pay the dollar tax on each of your gifts and you will be remembered as, ahem, history's greatest philanthropist. If you desire not to pay the tax, I'm sure your spirit will still remain with us ... and I speak for all Americans!"

At that point, members of the New Party applauded. The Democrat, Republican, Independent lawmakers sat on their hands. The crowd jeered.

"However, I'm saddened to say (as if he was) that you will not be permitted to enter our country unless you agree to pay the required tax of $1 on every gift you deliver.

"But, no matter what, the spirit of Christmas will remain, for we will have your likenesses on street corners collecting money for underprivileged families as well as greeting children in department stores."

Santa Claus paused before he spoke. "Senator, I've always been overjoyed to see my likeness on the streets and in department stores both here and in countries everywhere.

"They are indeed philanthropists, for they help the needy with their collections and bring smiles to the mouths of children.

"But, as for me, I am unable to pay your expensive tariff and will miss visiting the homes of American's children on the eve of this Christmas, tomorrow. It just won't be the same."

Santa shook in disbelief that this was happening.

He reached into his pocket to retrieve a huge red handkerchief and wiped tears from his eyes.

McGreedy was unmoved. It was time for him to damage Santa's reputation, and his star witness was ready.

"Mr. Claus," McGreedy began, "there is evidence that many of your toys are inferior to those produced by American companies and those in China. Is that true?"

"I know that *not* to be true," said Santa. He rose to his feet, then hit his clenched fist against the tabletop. His voice rose. "My helpers and I take great pride and enjoyment in making these magnificent gifts for children around the world. We receive millions of letters every year and not once, mind you, have we ever gotten a complaint."

"You're out of order, Mr. Claus," McGreedy shouted back. "Please sit down!" He turned to the man wearing the black pin-striped suit in the hearing room and said, "Mr. Fitch, would you kindly identify yourself?"

"Yes, Senator. I am president of Fitch & Mitch."

McGreedy decided to swear in Fitch himself.

"Do you plan to tell the truth, the whole truth, so help you God?"

"I do."

The Santa Claus Trial

"Please tell our Committee members your occupation."

"Fitch & Mitch is a New York City company hired by manufacturers to inspect the quality of products produced by their competition."

"What kind of products?"

"Electrical appliances, machinery, automobile parts and ..."

"And what else?" McGreedy asked.

"Toys, Senator."

"Ah, yes," said McGreedy as he leaned back in his chair. His moment had come. "Have you ever inspected Santa's toys?"

"Yes, I have."

"What did your research find, say, from a rating of 1 to 10?"

"Based on our company's rating system, we found Santa's toys to be in the 5 category, well below toys made in America and even in China."

The crowd in the gallery greeted Fitch with a chorus of boos.

McGreedy ignored them. Santa was noticeably upset and again quickly sprang from his chair and leaned in the direction of Fitch.

"Mr. Fitch," Santa said softly, "you haven't told

The Santa Claus Trial

the truth. I believe you know your testimony to be a lie. Heaven help you." He sat down.

A new voice spoke. It was Hawaiian Senator John Justice, who had attended law school at Harvard University and who had served in the House of Representatives before being elected to the Senate.

"Mr. Fitch, how long has your company been in business?" he inquired.

"Two years, sir," Fitch replied.

"Hmmm, two years. Seems to me you've gained lots of knowledge in a short period of time." It was obvious Justice was attempting to discredit Fitch's testimony.

"Yes, sir."

"If I may ask, how did you go about getting your final results?"

"We visited the homes of families who told us they had received gifts from Mr. Claus."

"How many families?"

"We didn't need too many. About a half-dozen."

"That seems like a ridiculously low number," Justice said. "I would expect an issue of this importance to call for visits to hundreds of homes and inspections of hundreds, even thousands, of Santa's toys. For the record, do you have the names of the families you visited, including the number of homes?"

The Santa Claus Trial

"I believe you know your testimony to be a lie."

"Yes, sir. Because we had little time to conduct the survey, we visited two homes where my grandchildren lived; three homes owned by my friends; and a neighbor's home."

"Did you ask your grandchildren if they were unhappy with the toys?"

"No, they were in school and I asked their parents for permission to inspect the gifts."

"Hardly a credible survey, Mr. Fitch. Wouldn't you agree?"

"Yes, but ... but ... Senator McGreedy contacted me only several days ago."

"So it was the senator who contacted you?"

"Yes."

"Interesting." Senator Justice thoughtfully rubbed his chin. "What did you do before you formed your company?"

Fitch seemed to be rattled. "I- I- was a quality-control inspector."

"Where?"

"At a candy company."

"Must have been a sweet job," quipped Justice. There was laughter in the room. "Are you a friend of Senator McGreedy?" he inquired.

"I object!" yelled McGreedy.

"All right, Senator, let me rephrase my question. Mr. Fitch, did you ever meet Senator McGreedy previously? Now, remember," Justice reminded him. "You've taken an oath."

"Yes, yes," Fitch began. "I met the good senator at a convention of the Toymakers and Retail Association of America in Cincinnati, Ohio, two years ago."

"Why did you attend this convention, which has nothing to do with the confection industry?"

"I was invited by my friend, who is president of the association. He thought it would be a good idea to meet the senator inasmuch as I was thinking about opening my own quality-control company."

"And what did the good senator tell you?"

"He encouraged me to establish my company."

"Senator McGreedy *encouraged* you? An interesting coincidence."

"Yes, and I am grateful to him."

"Guess that's why you're here?"

"Yes, yes," Fitch answered nervously. Drops of sweat ran down his forehead. Senator Justice's questioning had hit a nerve.

"You must be a genius, Mr. Fitch," Justice said, "Suddenly becoming an expert on a variety of products ... even Santa's toys. Remarkable."

Senator Justice looked around the hearing room. "Mr. Fitch, I find your testimony to be ingenuous and contrived. You have unjustly targeted Mr. Claus for reasons that are evident," he said as he glanced at McGreedy, for he too had heard about how corrupt the senator was.

"Mr. Claus," Justice said, "You have my vote and that of my colleagues. God bless you for all that you do to brighten the lives of our children everywhere on this most joyous holiday."

As Fitch returned to his seat, McGreedy looked directly at Justice. "Well, well, Senator, it appears you were attempting to discredit Mr. Fitch's testimony," said McGreedy angrily. "I don't think you succeeded," he grumbled. But, judging from the expression on the faces of many of the senators of both minority and majority parties, it appeared that Fitch's testimony had been far from convincing.

It was time for McGreedy to once again focus the committee's attention on Santa. "Mr. Claus, let's get on with your testimony. It appears to me and members of my party that you are a very rich man."

"I'm not sure what you mean," Santa responded.

"Well, sir, it must cost you a vast amount of money to produce all those children's gifts, dolls, doll houses, teddy bears, and even iPods and computers. So if you can afford to make those items, why can't you afford to pay our tax?"

Santa began, "I can only tell you that the price of making those gifts has risen dramatically. As a matter of fact, they're out of control, as you well know. We are always seeking ways to be more cost-effective. Don't let the color of my suit fool you; we're going green! Ho, Ho, Ho!" Once again Santa was amused by his wit and sought approval from the people in the gallery.

But he grew serious and continued. "Senator, our funding is limited, and if we were to spend even some of it to pay your proposed taxes, it would prevent me from visiting all the homes here on Christmas Eve. Is that what you want?"

There was a stunned silence. McGreedy was startled by Santa's frank rebuttal but didn't waste much time trying to convince the senators and the public in general that the tariff was needed.

"Dramatic rebuttal, Mr. Claus," he snickered. "I'm told your reindeer are able to fly only if they are fed a magic corn provided by some so-called 'wizard.' If that's true, why can't this *magical* gentleman provide the money for our tax?"

"I object!" said Kate. She stood up, raised her voice, and stared with contempt at McGreedy. "That, frankly, Senator, is a confidential matter and not any concern of yours or of anybody else in this room. This entire hearing is something you should be ashamed of! I am advising Mr. Claus to stop answering any more of your questions."

"You tell 'em, Kate!" a woman yelled from the gallery. Again, there was a loud round of applause.

"Oh, yes, he must answer, Mrs. Camper. He is under oath to tell the truth," McGreedy shouted back.

"Not if he takes the 5th Amendment," replied Kate.

Santa leaned toward Kate and asked what she meant. She said quietly, "It guarantees that you do not have to testify against yourself, and it protects you from abuse from evil men like McGreedy."

An impatient McGreedy once again pounded the gavel. "Mr. Claus, I'm waiting for an answer!"

"I'm taking the 5th Amendment, Senator."

The men, women and children in the gallery gave Santa a standing ovation.

"You're excused, Mr. Claus. I will ask the Senate to vote on the bill tomorrow," McGreedy said.

A thoroughly confused Santa rose from his chair and shook his head in disbelief.

"It's OK, Mr. Claus," Kate reassured him. "McGreedy hasn't heard the last from us."

They exited the Senate chamber. A disappointed Santa would return to the North Pole on Rodriquez's plane. The tariff bill was sure to receive all the votes needed to pass it.

But tomorrow, Senator Rightman's voice would be the last to be heard. Could he convince enough New Party members to change their votes?

And how about that mystery man who had called Camper earlier, telling him he had proof that McGreedy was breaking the law by taking gifts from members of the Toymakers and Retailers Association of America? Would he come forward and testify on behalf of Santa Claus? It's a fact that it is unlawful for any member of Congress to accept payments from persons or companies seeking to change or establish a law in their favor.

Note: The Kennedy Caucus Room is named in honor of Senators John F. Kennedy, Robert F. Kennedy, and Edward M. Kennedy. The room also became familiar to moviegoers as the setting for such classic Hollywood films as "Mr. Smith Goes to Washington" [1939] and "Advise and Consent" [1962].

Chapter 15

Senator Rightman Defends Santa Claus

Most senators were more than eager to head home for the Christmas holiday, rather than attending the special session called for December 24th, for the vote on the Santa Claus Tariff bill. But none dared to leave Washington because of the intense media coverage.

It is now 9 a.m. Eastern Standard Time, 8 a.m. in most Midwest cities and towns, and 6 a.m. on the West Coast. Many European cities are at least seven hours ahead. No matter the time, people across the United States and around the world had been watching the proceedings either on their TVs or their mobile devices. The world was awaiting the final outcome.

One hundred senators have prepared to cast their votes in a house truly divided. New Party members outnumber those of the minority parties and are seated separately, the chamber's aisle being the dividing line.

New Party Vice President Brad Bragger has taken his seat on the elevated platform. He is to preside over what many predict will be a stormy session. According to Senate rules, he must be referred to as "President."

Senator McGreedy sits at his desk, in the front row. Senator Rightman's seat is also in the front row, but on the other side of the aisle.

Bragger called the Senate to order. The speeches for and against the bill began, with many senators standing at their desks as they spoke.

It was finally Senator Rightman's turn. After being recognized, he rose from his chair and looked directly at McGreedy.

"Senator," he said. "We are shocked at the way you treated Mr. Claus yesterday. I feel ashamed of the manner in which you and the members of your New Party have behaved. I am not proud of the way you continue to use the floor of the Senate to smear individuals and their reputation. Until you and your party took office, the United States Senate had long enjoyed worldwide respect.

"I too realize that our government must control trade between other nations in order to economically support our citizens, but you have gone too far. You have invoked what really is an unreasonable tariff that prevents Santa Claus from bringing his toys to our country.

"Meanwhile, our government refuses to charge a comparable tariff to friendly countries like China, whose imports of cheap products continue to be a

The Santa Claus Trial

"We are shocked at the way you treated
Mr. Claus yesterday."

challenge to toy manufacturers here. I think you understand, Mr. Chairman."

Rightman paused here in purposeful reference to the rumored ties McGreedy has had with the Toymakers and Retailers Association of America.

"So, Senators," he continued, "I have the perfect solution: Let's increase the import taxes on China and other countries. If we do this, we can raise enough money and need not levy a tax against Mr. Claus."

"Brilliant, Senator," McGreedy mockingly replied as he slowly and loudly clapped his hands. "The fact of the matter is that if we raise taxes for these friendly countries, they in turn will raise taxes on the products we export to their countries."

At that point Bragger slammed the gavel and directed his remarks to McGreedy.

"Senator, you're out of order! Senator Rightman has the floor, and you can make your rebuttal after he finishes." Considering that Bragger is a member of the New Party, it was a bold move to temporarily silence the powerful McGreedy.

But McGreedy ignored Bragger's pronouncement. "Mr. President, I do believe I have every right to reply to Senator Rightman, who is attempting to assassinate my character. After all, it was I who introduced this bill, and it will be I who defends it!"

Bragger used the gavel again. "Senator, I hope you realize that you're going against the rules of the Senate by engaging in a debate with another senator who has the floor."

"Maybe so," McGreedy shouted, "but this bill is too important to let someone like Senator Rightman destroy it! Hang the protocol!"

"Well then, Senator Rightman, do you have any objections?" asked Bragger.

"No, no, let it be. Let's continue. If the senator does not think raising import taxes is a good idea, then why don't we tax countries currently permitted to import their goods freely? I will be glad to submit such a bill to our Senate colleagues and pass it on to members of the House of Representatives for their consideration. This bill should result in raising billions of dollars and eliminate the need to tax Santa Claus."

"Not necessary, Senator," McGreedy said caustically. "I know President Trublood wants to retain a status quo regarding those non-paying countries, and ..."

An angry Rightman interrupted. "You mean our President who has given America an economy during his term that has yet to have sea legs?"

"Mr. President," McGreedy said coolly, "I think we have had enough discussion on our proposed bill. I request a vote."

Rightman stood. "No, not yet Mr. President. There is something else I want to say. I will not yield the floor!"

Members of the gallery, who had been listening intently to the to-and-fro of the senators, applauded wildly.

McGreedy, obviously perturbed by Rightman's speech and the response from the gallery, once again asked Bragger to call for an immediate vote.

The cowardly Bragger, realizing he would not have been elected if it weren't for McGreedy, called for a vote.

At that exact moment, a New Party member surprisingly shouted from the floor, "Mr. President, let the senator speak!"

Bragger recovered and said, "Oh, all right. The floor is yours, Senator Rightman. Please make it quick."

"Thank you." Rightman paused and looked directly at McGreedy. "My colleagues and I, for good reason, are afraid that you and the senators representing your party will show Mr. Claus no mercy. I guess from the looks of things we're correct. It's a shame ... an injustice. You seem bent on destroying this wonderful and charitable man."

Glaring at members of the New Party, he continued. "I speak as a United States Senator, I speak as an American. By voting for this bill, you will have done an injustice not only to Santa Claus but also to the meaning of this wondrous holiday. You will also have destroyed this generous and most colorful gift giver, and the spirit of Christmas Day will never be the same for millions of our nation's children. You will have broken their hearts."

Rightman proceeded to single out two New Party members: Senators Charlie Cantdo and Harold Hardknocks. Though neither was an exceptionally bright public servant, both had been Senator Rightman's longtime friends until they switched from their respective political parties to jump aboard the New Party bandwagon during the 2016 elections. Rightman claimed they had abandoned their principles and their parties just so they could become re-elected. He had seldom spoken to them since.

"Charlie, you have five grandchildren, and Harold, you're the father of two teenagers. I know those adorable children, having met them on happier occasions. I'll bet that neither of you has had the courage to ask them if they favor this shameful bill.

"You probably have never asked them because you know in your hearts that the action taken by Senator McGreedy is ludicrous. You never asked them because you know what their answers will be."

Rightman continued, now aiming his remarks at McGreedy. "Many of us have read about the legendary

King Arthur and his Knights of the Round Table. In the story of Camelot, Arthur states that Might is right. That cannot be said for your own Knights of the Round Table, Senator McGreedy. To them, Might is evil!"

The crowd in the gallery roared its approval.

Bragger pounded his gavel. "Order! Order! Order!," he demanded.

McGreedy could not contain himself. "Do you have any other fairy tales to tell members of my party, Senator?"

"What I told you is not a fairy tale, but the truth—something I'm sure you find hard to believe," Rightman continued. "We all know that you have the votes to pass the Santa Tariff Act today, and by tonight the President will sign it. But you haven't heard the last from us. The men, women, and children up in the gallery represent the millions of families opposed to your bill. Yes, this may well be the end of a chapter, but not the end of the book!

"Unfortunately, the national elections are a year away and there will be no opportunity to repeal this bill immediately. However, we will not remain silent. We will make every effort to unseat you and members of your Party when the time comes. Beginning tomorrow, we shall take our fight with confidence and strength to the streets of our nation's cities and towns, to the churches and schools, to the farmlands. We will take our fight to the people and never give up until we bring justice to this great man. Mark my words, your New Party will become the 'Old Party.' That much I pledge to you!"

The crowd cheered.

"Poetic, Senator," McGreedy began with a sneer. "You obviously have a following, based on the reception you are getting from the people witnessing this hearing. Do you consider yourself a martyr?"

"No," Rightman responded. "I consider myself a patriot. I stand here for those who oppose you … those sitting here today who belong to minority parties…the Democrats, Republicans, and Independents. I stand here today for those courageous men and women sitting in the gallery. Their voices have already been heard in what has now become the darkness.

"Government is supposed to exist for the good of the people, not the other way around, and certainly not for the personal enrichment of those who hold public office, Senator McGreedy." Another dramatic pause.

"In 1903 a respected poet by the name of Edward Everett Hale—a relative of Nathan Hale, the soldier who gave his life in 1776 so that the Revolution could succeed—stood on this very Senate floor as its chaplain. I have always been inspired by his words:

'I am only one,
but I am one.
I cannot do everything,
but I can do something
What can I do
I ought to do
by God's graces
I WILL do.'

Rightman sat and then slumped in his chair as the people in the gallery stood to give him a thunderous ovation. So did the Democrats, Republicans, and Independents, as well as many more than expected from the New Party.

And so it happened that the Santa Tariff Act would pass the Senate's vote, but by a 57-43 margin, much closer than anyone could have expected. It was to be signed that evening by President Trublood.

Chapter 16

The Santa Revolution

Bill Camper, expecting the tariff bill to be headed toward President Trublood, had already started to write a column on the Internet encouraging people to protest immediately. It received overwhelming responses from the young and old across the United States and in countries overseas. Thousands of messages appeared on Twitter, Facebook and YouTube, many upset with the New Party and agreeing with Camper, who called for a Candlelight Vigil to be held that night in Lafayette Park, across from the White House.

The signing ceremony was purposely set for that time, on that date, Christmas Eve, by McGreedy, the man whose contempt for Santa Claus had gotten the better of any concern about America's children.

There were no cheers at the headquarters of the International Santa Workers Union, whose 45,000 professional members—all dressed as Santa Clauses—are employed in many of the world's department stores. An emergency meeting was held in Oslo, Norway, where the union's headquarters is situated. SWU's purpose is to make sure that its Santa members get properly paid for their services during the Christmas holidays.

The late evening session on December 23 had involved a dozen directors from different countries, Canada, Mexico, and Japan, among them. Hans Schmidt, the union's executive director, called the meeting to order and did not hesitate to begin a discussion regarding Santa's plight. Schmidt owned a butcher shop in Berlin, which his family managed while he played Santa each Christmas.

"It's terrible what is happening in America to Mr. Claus," he began. "I spoke with him a couple of days ago, and he is disappointed with the bill proposed by the U.S. Senate. He simply doesn't have the money to pay those taxes and does not want any contributions from the public. He's a proud man."

After hearing their opinions, Schmidt called for a vote. The delegate from Canada raised his hand and made a motion calling for a removal of Santas from all retail stores in the U.S. "This will show our solidarity with Mr. Claus," he said. The motion was seconded by the representative from Iceland. The vote was unanimous, and word spread quickly. It was the beginning of a nationwide boycott.

And so it was that department store Santas across America failed to report to work on Christmas Eve day.

The Santa Claus Trial

The International Santa Workers Union called for a nationwide strike.

The Santa Claus Trial

The news had not reached 76-year-old Patrick "Paddy" O'Brien, Jack Sr.'s neighbor. He had retired from the steel mill and looked forward to each Christmas holiday so he could once again play Santa Claus at Holman's Department Store.

But today would be different.

Paddy arrived at the store just before noon and headed to its employee cafeteria. He enjoyed a hot cup of coffee there before getting ready to move the ornate Santa chair where eager youngsters would tell him what Christmas gifts they wanted.

"Paddy, I see you've had your morning coffee," owner Eric Holman said as he sat down. "That's good, because you're going to need to stay awake today."

Holman, tall and slender, was known for his immaculate appearance. He wore expensive suits and shirts and colorful bow ties. His slick black hair was neatly coiffed, a work of art for the lady's man he still considered himself to be, despite a wife and children. Earlier, he had been delighted to find out that the Santa Tariff Act had been approved by the Senate.

"Never close my eyes, Mr. Holman. Why is this day different than any other day?"

"Haven't you heard the news?"

"Can't say I have. Don't have time for that nonsense. Are the Bears playing this week?"

Paddy frequently forgot to check his mail or read a newspaper. He had no use for the Internet. His hours of television were devoted to sports programming, including watching his beloved Cubs play in the summer and Bears in the fall and winter.

"Don't follow football," Holman snapped.

"Too bad, that's where all the action is … not here," Paddy quipped. "So what are you all excited about?"

"The Senate passed the Santa Tariff Act this morning, and that means that your namesake will no longer be able to deliver his gifts to our children."

"That's terrible, but I'm not surprised. Bill Camper predicted as much," Paddy said evenly.

Holman could barely contain himself. "On the contrary, this means that millions of parents are going to have to replace Santa's gifts by coming to stores like ours. I expect to see a long line of customers waiting to get inside before midnight, hired extra guards to control the traffic. Let's face it, Paddy, you're going to be a popular Santa today. Let's go to work!"

"You shouldn't be so happy, Mr. Holman."

"Why not? We're holding a huge inventory of toys, smartphones, tablets, televisions, the latest clothing, and all kinds of other things. If all goes as well as I think it will, we'll unload all of that and more

… and we may be able to give you a raise, maybe even hire more Santas!"

Paddy suddenly let loose.

"I've known your family for a long time and have always been grateful to your father for giving me this job, Eric, but I'm disappointed in you. You sided with that crazy senator and the low-life people who belong to that organization you always talk about. I'll bet they're also celebrating … big time. You ought to be ashamed of yourself. I'm sure your father is turning over in his grave.

Holman's face registered shock.

"Furthermore, I'm not interested in a raise. Margaret and I saved enough money so we would not have to depend on our children or anyone else for support. I only keep this job to keep myself busy.

"Maybe you forgot, but I was young when my parents came to this country without much money. My father took any kind of job he could get in order to put food on the table. I never was a scholar; I dropped out of high school to help support my family and eventually got that job in the steel mill … not a fancy job like the one your father gave you. Guess rich folks like you look down on people like me."

"Paddy, that's just not true," Holman said. "I mean, the more sales we make, the more people we can hire. Is that so bad?"

Paddy ignored Holman's statement. He was on fire. "We came to America because it was a land of opportunity. It still is ... but justice? How in the heck could those politicians in Washington pass a bill stopping Santa Claus from coming to America on Christmas Eve? Yes, Eric, children will find gifts under their Christmas trees tomorrow morning, but it won't be the same."

With a sigh, Paddy got up and walked the short distance to the raised platform where his chair was located. His cell phone rang as he sat down.

It was a call from Louie Sharp, the local union steward for the International Santa Workers Union.

"Paddy, what the heck are you doing, playing Santa Claus at Holman's?"

"What do ya mean?"

"I mean the union has called for a strike. We're not puttin' up with that slime-ball senator and those disgraceful New Party idiots who passed that bill this morning. We're all for one and one for all! So get your tail up and out of the store!"

"No need to say more, Louie. I'm out!" Paddy arose from his chair, startling the children lined up waiting to talk to him. He nodded at them somewhat apologetically before heading for the door. Eric Holman stopped him.

"Where are you going, Paddy? We've got children waiting for you!"

"I can assure you, Eric, that you're probably seeing the last of those children at your store, especially when word gets around that you've supported McGreedy and his gang. No sir, we Santas are not stooges! Farewell!"

And out the door he went.

Chapter 17

A Moment of Truth

 It is early morning this December 24. Nightfall will bring with it the President's signing of the Santa Tariff Act. For the first time ever, Santa Claus will not visit homes in the United States.

Senator McGreedy ordered President Trublood to schedule the signing of the Santa Tariff Bill (# 122419) in the Oval Office at the White House at 8 p.m. Eastern Standard Time on Christmas Eve.

Aside from McGreedy, the dramatic ceremony is to be attended by some of his cronies, including Senators Wishwashee, Whimpers and Takers, as well as Susan Simpler, the Speaker of the House. Several Cabinet members will also be present.

McGreedy took charge. His press secretary, Ted Downs, alerted the media of this historic signing that would keep Santa Claus from entering the United States Christmas Eve.

Unless there is a miracle at the 11th hour, it is a sure bet Santa cannot afford to raise the money he needs to pay the unreasonable tariff.

Strong-minded McGreedy will make sure that nothing prevents the weak President from placing his signature on the bill.

In the meantime, Kate and Camper have decided to remain in Washington, where they will continue their fight against McGreedy.

The couple pleaded for men, women, and children everywhere to attend the Candlelight Vigil and to gather at Lafayette Park this evening to show support for this jolly old man who brings to the world the generosity and warmth of the human spirit.

Then, around 2 p.m., the call Camper had been waiting for finally came.

It was the mysterious man who finally identified himself as Albert Hubka, a member of the Toymakers and Retailers Association of America's board of directors. He told Camper that he was present when the board approved an agreement that would give McGreedy one million dollars, providing the Santa Tariff Act was approved by the Senate and signed by the President. The funds would be transferred to an offshore bank so no one could trace them. Hubka said he was the only person who did not vote for the agreement.

"I went back inside and took a picture of the document with my camera when our directors left the room for a coffee break," he said. "I also have a video showing the senator bragging about what he was going

The Santa Claus Trial

"How fast can you get to Washington?"

to do to prevent Santa Claus from coming to America and possibly other countries. It was taken at the airport just before he boarded his plane for Washington."

"How fast can you get to Washington?" asked Camper.

"I live in Charlotte, North Carolina and will have to drive in; planes are grounded due to bad weather here. Should be there in four hours or so."

"Are you willing to show the documentation to the press?"

"Yes, yes, of course. I want nothing to do with TRAA any longer," Hubka said.

"OK, we'll call a press conference for around 6 p.m. Contact me from time to time, and I will direct you to my hotel."

"Will do. Good bye!"

After hanging up, Camper ran into the next room where Kate was working the Internet. "Hey, baby, I think Santa Claus is coming to town!"

"What do you mean?" she asked.

"We got the guy who will tell the American public what a scoundrel McGreedy really is. Hey, there's no way the President will sign that bill once we prove that the senator was in bed with the toymakers and retailers. I really don't think Trublood knew of McGreedy's unlawful dealings.

"I'm going to call Stuffy and tell him the good news. This is one heck of a scoop for us… and welcome news for American families!"

Chapter 18

Albert Hubka's Demise

Camper remained in his hotel suite with Kate and was not going to notify reporters of the pending press conference until he had reviewed Hubka's video and document indicating that McGreedy was being paid by the Toymakers and Retailers Association of America to stop Santa Claus from entering the United States.

But he was getting worried. It had been more than five hours since Camper had first spoken to Hubka. Only hours remained before Trublood would make the Santa Tariff Act official. It was 7:30 p.m. Where is Hubka?

Suddenly, Camper's cell phone rang. It was from State Trooper Michael Wong. "Mr. Camper," he said, "I have some bad news. A person identified as 45-year-old Albert Hubka has died of injuries suffered when his car overturned on Interstate 95."

"What! How did this happen?" asked Camper.

"Witnesses tell us that his car was sideswiped by a pickup truck. We believe that caused him to lose control of his car, which ended up in a ditch. We were also told that a man stepped out of the truck and ran

The Santa Claus Trial

"I have some bad news."

to the car. A few minutes later he was seen running back with a package. None of the witnesses were able to give us a license number."

"How did you know to call me?"

"When we looked for his identification, we found a note in his jacket pocket."

"Please read it."

"Yes, sir. It said, 'Please contact reporter Bill Camper in case anything happens to me.' It contained your phone number, sir. Sorry."

"Thank you," Camper said before he hung up.

Kate entered the room and noticed a dejected Camper sitting on the edge of his bed, his head bowed, still clutching his cell phone.

"Bill, what's the matter?"

"We've lost our star witness. Hubka must have known his life was in danger."

"What do you mean?"

He told her of his conversation with the state trooper. "I think someone knew Hubka was on his way to Washington and wanted to make sure he never reached his destination. It looks like the evidence was taken from the car. He was murdered."

"Murdered," Kate gasped. "Who do you think is responsible for his death?"

"I don't believe McGreedy, as malicious as he is, would know about my conversation with Hubka, or even take part in such a heinous crime. It has to be someone from the Toymakers and Retailers Association of America, and my bet the orders came from its president, Marty Mischief, who has Mob ties."

Camper's theory was correct. Mischief had recognized that Hubka disapproved of the scam he had cooked up with Senator McGreedy and had had his phones tapped. After hearing the conversation with Camper, he hired two thugs to trail Hubka and, at the opportune moment, sideswipe his car and seize the evidence.

There was no way Camper could ever prove his theory, but that would not prevent him from using Social media to report the tragic incident and the nation's disappointment in the passing of the Santa Tariff Act.

He wrote the following: "Earlier today, the Senate approved a bill that prevents Santa Claus from coming to the United States. The signing ceremony for the Santa Tariff Act has been purposely scheduled minutes away from Christmas Eve by a senator who has constantly shown contempt for this jolly old man and little concern for the millions of children who have waited all year for his arrival.

"Mr. Claus has returned to his home in the North Pole and is making preparations for his flight to homes everywhere around the world, except the United States. As was reported recently, my son, Brandon, and pilot Ricky Rodriguez, spent some refreshing hours with this warm and witty gift giver. We know his heart is broken.

"Those of us who are old enough to vote and those of you who are too young to have this privilege just now, must understand that all politicians are not created equal. There are the good, the bad, the not-so-bad serving the public on a local or national scale. And then there is the New Party... the evil.

"Senator Travis McGreedy and House Speaker Susan Simpler collaborated and played significant roles in passing the Santa Tariff Act, much to the regret and disappointment of American families and people around the globe. Unfortunately, the New Party had the control of Congress and there was little anyone could have done to defeat this dreadful bill.

"One lawmaker fought to save our Santa. He is Minority Leader Josh Rightman. He is a patriot. On this darkest morning, he brought the country some sunshine. And there is another hero, Albert Hubka, who was on his way this afternoon to bring me evidence that proved the Toymakers and Retailers Association of America had paid Senator McGreedy to create a bill that would prevent Santa Claus from coming to America and bring huge profits to their membership for years to come.

The Santa Claus Trial

"Earlier today, the Senate approved a bill …."

"Mr. Hubka never made it to my hotel room in Washington. He was killed in a suspicious car accident on Highway 295 near Petersburg, Virginia.

Chapter 19

President Trublood Confronts McGreedy

It is the night before Christmas and America is stirring.

Camper's articles calling for a vigil for Santa appear to be effective. Hundreds arrived early at Lafayette Park, some setting up tents.

Father McCloskey and Rev. Jordan are also early arrivals. They have brought with them members of their respective church choirs who expect to sing the traditional Christmas carols in front of the White House's Oval Office, where the signing ceremony will take place.

Each had selected the twenty best voices for the trip, all with diversified backgrounds. Twenty-eight-year-old grocery clerk Willie Johnson, for instance, likes to sing in the shower and still does. His family convinced him to take his talent to Rev. Jordan's church. Tina Snow, 38, was glad she was selected for the trip. The Mississippi housewife and mother of four said she wanted to do her part to convince the President to veto the bill. "Lord, my kids will be disappointed if

Santa doesn't visit our home."

Maria De Luca's star shines. The tall, slender, bespectacled woman is wearing a flowered dress that reaches down to her ankles and is partially covered by her gray winter coat. At 66, she remains a captivating soprano whose voice is still magnificent. By far, she is Father McCloskey's brightest voice.

Maria's parents were first-generation immigrants of Italian descent. She began taking voice lessons at the age of 8 and later performed with many light-opera companies. She never married and works part-time in a library near the church.

"We hope the President will hear these wonderful songs that remind all of us of the true meaning of Christmas and veto the Santa Tariff Act," said Father McCloskey.

"Amen," added the Rev. Jordan. "Lord, we want our Santa Claus!"

As the sun disappeared and the moon took its place, thousands crowded the streets alongside the White House and adjacent Lafayette Park carrying candles that lit the darkness. There were men, women, and children of all ages, many holding signs asking Trublood to veto McGreedy's unpopular bill.

There were also others present, including people from different religious denominations, many of whom don't celebrate this Christian holiday but who came to show their support. There were the elderly in wheel chairs, those struggling to take steps with their walkers, and mothers pushing their babies in carriages this late evening. There were people of all races with hearts beating true to the red, white and blue.

Also among them the dozens of identically dressed Santa Clauses who refused to return to their respective department stores, led by none other than old Patrick O'Brien. He had left Chicago the day before in his Winnebago motor home loaded with boxes of candles that were to be distributed to those attending this dramatic event. His passengers in the large van were his wife, Mary, and the elder Campers and their granddaughter, Sara. Soon after they arrived, Brandon reached them by cell phone and joined them in the park.

But this was not only happening in Washington. Millions gathered in the streets and parks of cities and towns throughout the United States, showing their support for Santa as they held their own vigils. There were similar ceremonies in several countries overseas.

TV networks were busy filming this momentous happening, and families who could not take part in a vigil stood by their televisions.

Meanwhile, at the North Pole, Santa was taking a nap after being fed a sumptuous meal by Mrs. Claus. Elves were busy loading bundles of gifts onto his large sleigh that would carry him on his flight to homes around the world. Santa wasn't giving up and had bundles of toys set aside for a possible trip to the U.S., even though the likelihood of that happening appeared highly improbable.

Action at the White House also picked up steam. President Trublood, who had been on a goodwill trip to Europe, spoke to members of his Cabinet from inside Air Force One, which was just leaving London after a long delay.

Trublood, showing a little spunk, informed his secretary he wanted the signing ceremony to be a private event and ordered that only the White House official photographer be present in the Oval Office, located on the second floor in the West Wing.

"The American public is against this unpopular Santa Tariff Act and sometimes I too have second thoughts about signing it." he said. "My wife and children are critical of the bill. Nonetheless, I promised Senator McGreedy long ago that I would approve such a bill if elected President... and I will.

"Let the reporters know I will meet them afterward in the Briefing Room, where I will outline the reasons for the need to sign the bill," he said.

Trublood's decision to soften the blow to the American public was not taken lightly by McGreedy, who had wanted some hand-picked correspondents and TV networks present at the signing ceremony. He contacted the President, who was already in flight.

"Morton, I think you should reconsider your

The Santa Claus Trial

"I believe this is the best approach."

decision to downplay this important occasion," said McGreedy sternly.

"I have, Travis, and I believe this is the best approach. I will make a short statement in the Briefing Room. That should suffice."

"You're making a mistake, Morton, and I'll make sure you pay for it in the coming election! Good bye!"

Trublood's late return resulted in McGreedy's moving the signing ceremony to 11 p.m. Santa's chances to enter the U.S. with his bundles of joy depended on whether President Trublood could arrive in Washington on time. If inclement weather delays his flight, there was a good chance he wouldn't reach the nation's capital by midnight.

Chapter 20

Here We Come A-Caroling

The temperatures had warmed considerably this winter day of reckoning, moving up from the cold 'teens during the early morning to about 35 degrees Fahrenheit by early afternoon and slightly dropping by nightfall. The moon once again stuck its head out of the gray clouds as the crowd of protestors grew to more than a half-million, according to estimates by the National Park Service police. The majority stood holding lit candles in Lafayette Park.

Camper had arranged for a 14-foot-wide wooden platform to be erected at the park. It was completed with the help of several former department store Santa Clauses and their grandsons, who had experience in constructing scaffolds similar to this one. A public address system, similarly rigged up, would enable Camper to speak to the immense crowd.

Father McCloskey and Rev. Jordan moved their respective church choirs to the south gate of the White House later than expected after learning about President Trublood's tardy arrival. They were confronted by a tall, husky, middle-aged man wearing a standard police uniform with a Presidential seal on his shoulder patch and a communications earpiece. He was a member of the Secret Service Uniform Division responsible for patrolling the grounds.

"Merry Christmas," said the Rev. Jordan.

"Same to you, sir," replied the tall, husky policeman.

"We are here to sing Christmas carols to the President and his family on this most joyous evening."

"Do you have an official invite?" the policeman asked.

"No," replied the Rev. Jordan.

"That's thoughtful, Reverend. I'm sure the President would really like to hear those songs, but I have to abide by the rules. Sorry."

Just then, Father McCloskey returned with one of the choir boys who had wandered from the group and gotten lost. "We're not allowed to enter the White House property," Rev. Jordan whispered in Father McCloskey's ear.

"Who said so?"

Rev. Jordan pointed to the guard. "He did!"

Him? Why ... why that must be Walter Slimski's son, John. I'd recognize that face anywhere. Use to be a choir boy in my church when I was a young priest, before I left for the Navy. A pretty good Little League player, too. Grown into a man, by golly." Father McCloskey approached him.

"Hello, John. How are you?"

The expression on the policeman's face was one of amazement as he recognized the priest. "Father McCloskey!?"

"Yes, we've both grown a little older, but you still have that twinkle in your eyes. I suppose you're married and have a family. And how are your parents?"

"Yeah, three teenagers, all growing up … fast! My dad passed away, but mom is still with us. We missed you, but I heard you were back at another church."

"Yes, that's true. My friend here, the Reverend Robert Jordan, was also a Navy Chaplain. John, how about letting us in for just a few minutes to sing Christmas carols to President Trublood and his family? If I remember correctly, you were never afraid to take chances. Please give us this opportunity."

"Sounds like you're up to something, Father."

"Yes, we want to save Santa. We're all praying and we hope our music, these Christmas poems, may once again remind the President that this holiday is a celebration of an historical tradition that brings with it hopes for peace and goodwill—not the destruction of Santa Claus. Well, enough of my preaching. What say you, John?"

"Just a moment, Father," John answered. He walked away from the group and could be seen holding his hand to his earpiece. Several minutes later he returned.

"Father, I spoke with the Chief, who said he would make an exception just this once because it is Christmas Eve; he will alert the other agents of your presence." John swung the gate open.

"All right Father. If the truth be known, the Chief, like the rest of us, is no fan of Senator McGreedy. But we are here for security purposes and must keep our political beliefs to ourselves. Merry Christmas."

"God bless you, son."

John waved the choir members into the White House grounds, and they headed toward the southeast section beneath the windows of the Oval Office, where President Trublood was expected to sign the bill.

After reaching the location, the clergymen quickly lined up both choruses, who were prepared to sing the following carols: *Deck the Halls with Boughs of Holly, Away in a Manger, Angels We Have Heard on High, The First Noel, God Rest Ye Merry, Gentlemen, Jingle Bells, Joy to the World, O Come All Ye Faithful, O Holy Night, Silent Night,* and O *Little Town of Bethlehem.*

Their voices would be heard.

The Santa Claus Trial

Their voices would be heard.

Chapter 21

The Beginning of the End

Camper's hopes of stopping the enactment of the Santa Tariff Act had all but vanished now that his star witness, Albert Hubka, was dead. However, if Trublood's plane arrived after midnight, it would be too late for him to sign the bill and prevent Santa from entering homes in the U.S.

Unfortunately, that wasn't the case.

Air Force One arrived in Washington at 10:30 p.m. Shortly afterward, he was in the Presidential helicopter and on his way to the lawn of the White House, where he was greeted by an impatient McGreedy.

"Morton, we don't have much time, so it's best if you change your casual clothes as soon as possible so we can get on with the ceremony before it's too late," he urged as they walked toward the White House door.

"Shouldn't be a problem. What time is it now?"

"Five minutes to eleven," answered McGreedy. "Hurry, the clock is ticking!"

Trublood departed for his living quarters on the

third where he hurriedly changed into a business suit, shirt, and plain red tie. He entered the Oval Office at 11:18 p.m., ready to sign the bill. The White House's official photographer, several Congressional leaders and Cabinet members were now present.

But they weren't alone. The choir below them was tuning up. Rev. Jordan, acting as choir director, waved his hands and the caroling began with *Joy to the World*. The song—one of many—was sure to be heard by the President.

"Who let those people on the White House grounds?" an irritated McGreedy demanded to know. "Get them out of here right now!" he screamed at Ted Downs, the White House press secretary.

"Yes, sir!" replied Downs, who ran to his office and picked up the phone, dialing the Chief. "Senator McGreedy wants you to remove those singers from these grounds ASAP!"

John Slimski had already revealed that McGreedy had no fans among members of the Secret Service serving the White House, including himself. Count the Chief in. He did not want to remove the choir and told the press secretary he was having difficulty in communicating with him.

"Hey, Ted, kinda difficult to hear you, barely can understand what you're saying. I'm having trouble with my phone, lots of static. Will get back to you as soon as I can."

The Santa Claus Trial

"Senator McGreedy is not going to like this!"

"What did you say?" asked the Chief.

"Oh, *nothing!* I have to get back to the Senator!" He hung up and rushed back to the Oval Office, telling McGreedy what had transpired.

"Hogwash! I'll go out there and get rid of those do-gooders myself!"

"Hold your horses," Trublood calmly said as he grabbed McGreedy's arm, stopping him from leaving the room. "I enjoy listening to the music. Remember, Travis, we're not losing the spirit of this holiday, just getting rid of a stubborn Santa Claus who doesn't want to help our economy by paying his share."

It was obvious the naïve President did not know the real purpose behind McGreedy's deceitful creation of his bill.

"Serves as a beautiful and inspirational musical background for our signing ceremony. Do all of you agree?" he turned and asked those who had come to witness the signing.

"I can speak for all of us here Mr. President," answered Susan Simpler. "We like the Christmas music, don't we?" she asked the other guests.

She was greeted by a smattering of applause. At that very moment the caroling was interrupted by crowds outside the White House chanting loudly for McGreedy's resignation.

The Santa Claus Trial

Trublood, ignoring the roar of disapproval, moved to his chair and sat down to read the contents of the bill. After several moments he said, "Well, it's close to midnight, and we'd better get going before it's too late to stop Mr. Claus from coming to America."

All the lawmakers gathered around his desk. As he lifted the first of several pens he was using to sign the document, he could hear an exchange of harsh words between a woman and Secret Service agents in the hallway outside the Oval Office.

"What's all the commotion about?" the President asked an agent.

"It's your daughter, Mr. President. She insists on seeing you."

"By all means, let her in!"

"Sign the damn bill!" growled McGreedy. At that moment, Trublood's daughter, Kristie, entered holding the hands of her two young children, Sandra, 5, and Randy, 7. "Dad, you can't sign that bill!"

"Why?"

"Why?" she screamed. "Bill Camper, that's why! His column was placed on Twitter an hour ago. He wrote that a man was murdered before he could bring him evidence that THAT man," she pointed to McGreedy, "was given money and gifts by the Toymakers and Retailers Association of America to destroy Santa!"

The Santa Claus Trial

"Absurd!" retorted McGreedy. "A bad rumor, Morton. Get on with it!"

"Absurd?" Kristie fired back. "Listen to the voices of those people outside who have just learned of Camper's report!"

Sandra rushed to the President's side and grabbed his leg. "Grandpa," she started crying, "Please, please let Santa come to America!"

Trublood patted her on the head and looked at Randy. "Do you feel the same way?"

"Yes, Grandpa, I do," he said solemnly. "Christmas isn't the same without Santa Claus."

"Sign the bill, Morton!" McGreedy again demanded.

"Shut up!" Trublood replied angrily. "I think Randy is right. What is Christmas without a real Santa Claus? No, Travis, I'm not signing the Santa Tariff Act." Trublood reached down and picked up the bill from the desk and stood face-to-face with McGreedy.

"Travis, I was a fool to believe that you had our country's interest when you and the others in our party brought this bill to the Senate floor…. and that includes you, Susan, and the rest of the 'gang' here. I suspect there was another reason for this legislation and will ask an impartial Ethics Committee for an investigation. Please leave this room. Now, the Santa Tariff Act is no longer an issue, and if you don't believe me, watch!"

Trublood waved the bill angrily back and forth and to their astonishment tore it to pieces.

"I'll see you don't get re-elected," yelled McGreedy as he left the Oval Office with the others.

"I'm not running for office next year!" Trublood shouted back. He wrapped his arms around Kristie and her two children, walking them to the window where they looked down as they listened to the delightful Christmas songs. "Lovely music," he mused. "You saved Santa. Thank you, my children, and God bless you."

Trublood grabbed pieces of the bill, slid the Oval Office window open, and threw the scraps of paper down toward the clergymen and their choir. "Here's what happened to the Santa Tariff Act!" he yelled. "Merry Christmas!"

Rev. Jordan was quick to bend down and recover several of the pieces. He looked up at Trublood as he held them tightly in one hand. "Thank you, Mr. President, and Merry Christmas to you and your family!"

He lifted both arms in the air and as he faced his choir and cried out as if he was on his pulpit of his church, "Hallelujah!"

As if on cue, the choir responded with three resounding and rhythmic "Hallelujahs" from Handel's

Messiah.

Father McCloskey pointed to his choir and they replied with an equally loud, "Amen!"

The clergymen shook hands. "We did it," said Rev. Jordan.

"Yes, we did, but we have to credit Bill Camper and Senator Josh Rightman, too. They were on the front lines. Guess we should be getting back to Lafayette Park."

Journalists covering the White House scrambled to their laptops and cell phones. Word of the President's action spread like wildfire around the world. Overjoyed crowds huddled on the streets by the Capitol Building and White House. Camper held Kate's hand as they hurriedly ran to mount the platform and address the people who had gathered in Lafayette Park for the candlelight vigil.

Meanwhile, Father McCloskey and Rev. Jordan were leading their choirs across the street to the park. "And let's say a prayer while we are there," Father McCloskey suggested.

Camper and Kate were now seen on the platform. He embraced Kate. "It's truly a miracle. Must call Santa and tell him he's coming to America after all!" He pulled the phone from his pocket.

Camper contacted Santa at his warehouse, where the elves had already loaded bundles of gifts on his sleigh for delivery to other countries, none marked for homes in America. Upon hearing the good news from Camper, he urged the elves to quickly add the bundles addressed for the United States.

Santa expressed his gratitude to Camper, Kate, Senator Rightman and the American people for their courageous campaign on his behalf.

"Getting a late start, though, Bill," he said as he hopped aboard his sleigh. "Ho, Ho, Ho! Merry Christmas! All right, Rudolph," he said as he took hold of the reins. "Lead the way!" he commanded. And within seconds, Santa and his reindeer disappeared into the darkness of night.

The huge crowd was still buzzing as Father McCloskey and the Rev. Jordan climbed the sturdy wooden stairs leading to the platform. Camper held the portable microphone in his hand, his voice bellowing through the loudspeakers. "Ladies and gentlemen… boys and girls. May I have your attention?"

The noise slowly simmered as he continued. "By now many of you have heard that President Trublood did *not* sign the Santa Tariff Act. As a matter of fact, he tore it up!"

The crowd broke out in thunderous cheers and applause.

"I just talked to Santa, and he wants to thank you for your support throughout this entire ordeal. Kate and I recommend you all go to your homes and

The Santa Claus Trial

"Maria DeLuca's voice and range
were mesmerizing."

have a good night's sleep. Santa is on his way to America!"

Camper handed the microphone to Father McCloskey. "Mr. Camper asked for a candlelight vigil to pray for Santa, and he got a darn good turnout! So please join us for a minute of silence to thank the Lord."

The people listened and obeyed. The silence was broken by a tall, angelic woman wearing a long flowered dress. Yes, it was Maria DeLuca. Her silver hair showed prominently under the park's lights. She started to sing the first two lines of *Hark! The Herald Angels Sing*. Her voice and range were mesmerizing:

"Hark! The herald angels sing

Glory to the newborn king....

Choir members followed suit, and hundreds of voices spontaneously joined in. Gradually, a crescendo of thousands of other voices was heard, including that of Senator Rightman, who mingled with the crowd, holding his three-year-old grandson on his shoulders.

The two New Party members Rightman had scolded during his speech in the Senate defending Santa Claus, Senators Cantdo and Hardknocks, surprisingly stood at his side, singing with their own families.

They were not alone. All of America also seemed to be giving voice to this notable carol, many following this dramatic turn of events on their tablets, radios, and televisions.

Spirits were high among the young and old who continued to remain in the park. Midnight was only minutes away. As people sang, dark clouds curtained the moon and a light snow began to fall.

Churches chimed in. The sound of bells rang throughout the land.

Rukia B. watched the celebration on TV from her cousin's apartment in Detroit, Michigan. She had recently been given permission to immigrate to the United States. Do you remember who Rukia is? She is the Iraqi teacher who earlier wrote a letter to Santa Claus. A charitable organization will pay for her son's surgery. He will be given an artificial leg.

She too began to sing:

> *"Hark! The herald angels sing,*
> *Glory to the newborn King,*
> *Peace on Earth, and mercy mild,*
> *God and sinners reconciled!*
> *Joyful, all ye nations rise,*
> *Join the triumph of the skies;*
> *With the Angelic host proclaim,*
> *Christ is born in Bethlehem."*

The Santa Claus Trial

Thousands gathered at St. Peter's Square.

Chapter 22

The Blessing

What could be more satisfying than an appropriate ending to a not-so-ordinary Christmas story? And what could be better than Santa Claus receiving a blessing from the Pope on Christmas Day as he is about to approach the North American continent, where most computers and televisions were shut down after midnight? Santa Claus, Kris Kringle, Father Christmas—take your pick—had already delivered his gifts to children in London, Paris, Rome and other European cities, towns and villages.

It was early morning when thousands gathered at St. Peter's Square. On Facebook, Twitter, by telephone and neighbor they had heard of Santa's victory over the evil senator and learned that the Pope was going to deliver a special prayer for this legendary gift-giver before rendering his traditional Christmas blessing. While the faithful waited for their spiritual leader to step onto the balcony, you could hear them chanting "Babbo Natale! Babbo Natale!" ("Father Christmas! Father Christmas!")

It wasn't long before the Pope made his appearance. He had prayed privately for divine

The Santa Claus Trial

"Babbo Natale!"

guidance for Santa and lighted a candle in a window overlooking the Square. Although he deplored the commercialism of the religious holiday and urged the faithful to look beyond its "superficial glitter" and to "never forget the true meaning of Christmas," he was excited about Santa's win in America and called it a "miracle".

The Pope, still wearing his garments from the Christmas Eve mass at St. Peter's Basilica, appeared fresh, even sprightly. He waved to the crowd and stepped to the microphone. His pronouncement was short but loud: "Babbo Natale!"

The crowd roared its response: "Babbo Natale!"

The Pope smiled as he repeated his proclamation.

The assembled wanted him to know they shared his joy and again answered "Babbo Natale!"

The pontiff made a slight turn and raised his hands and staff toward the sky. His gesture was symbolic of a noble blessing. "Santa Claus!" he shouted in English. "Miracola del miracoli!"

A miracle indeed.

Merry Christmas, Santa. Have a safe flight!

The Santa Claus Trial

THE END

The Santa Claus Trial

Notes:

The lyrics for "Hark! The Herald Angels Sing" were written in the 18th century by Charles Wesley; the music was composed by Felix Mendelssohn the following century.

The "Messiah" was written by German composer George Frederic Handel in 1741.

Santa left a note for Lisa and her mother thanking them for the skim milk and diet cookies. He did stop by the homes in that small town in Mexico and left gifts for Silva and her underprivileged friends. Ammar had successful surgery and now walks with a prosthesis instead of crutches. Sara received some extra dolls. And Brandon got a laptop computer, which he is using to write for his school's monthly newsletter.

The International Toymakers Council in Brussels withdrew its invitation to Senator McGreedy.

Senator Travis McGreedy was found guilty by members of the Ethics Committee, fined and reprimanded for his unsavory behavior.

The New Party was soundly defeated in a national election the following year and no longer held a majority in the House of Representatives. Senator McGreedy was not re-elected.

Senator Josh Rightman was elected President of the United States, succeeding Morton Trublood who retired and moved to his organic farm in Michigan.

Bill Camper was eventually promoted to Managing Editor of the Daily Sunlight after Stuffy Levine announced his retirement.